The Door in The Tree

Wicked on the Wind
Book 1

Alison Jean Ash

For Julie

[signature: Alison Jean Ash]

Look for Alison Jean Ash's other titles
You're So Vain, Comfort and Joy, Heart of Stone,
Welcome to Oakville (Anthology), A Mystery for
Marissa, and The Monday Mystery Society (Anthology)

ISBN-13:978-1515298205

ISBN-10:1515298205

Magpies

One for sorrow, two for joy,
Three for a girl and four for a boy,
Five for silver, six for gold,
Seven for a secret never to be told,
Eight for a wish, nine for a kiss,
Ten for the bird you must not miss.

Traditional English rhyme

Chapter One

March 2015
Stow-on-the-Wold, Gloucestershire, England

Even though she'd last seen it eighteen years ago—half her lifetime—Cecily recognized the enchanted tree at first glance. She stepped off the sidewalk to pause beneath the fine old oak. Every twig ended in a tiny dark red bud, no leaves yet. Spring came late this year.

A wicked little gust of wind touched her face and neck with icy fingers, and blew strands of her yellow hair across her eyes. A magpie flew away with a hoarse caw as Cecily looked up. She turned up her collar and shivered, but she would not let the chill drive her away.

The tree stood beside a garden wall, in a quiet curving street of honey-colored stone houses. It might not be as ancient as the thousand-year-old Tortworth Chestnut, but it was surely very old, much older than the house beyond the wall.

Why had she decided that this particular tree was magic? Studying it now, she noted the welcoming curve of its lower branches, the suggestion of a wise, kindly face in the whorls of the bark, the humped roots forming a lap at the base of the trunk. It was easy to see how an unhappy child might find it comforting.

But it had meant more to her than comfort. Cecily had always seen enchantment in it. She'd never gone past her tree without stopping to greet it, and on days of exceptional misery she'd go right behind it, where she couldn't be seen from the street. She'd lean into its gnarled trunk like a child at her grandmother's knee (though she'd never known either grandmother), look up into its branches, press her palms to its rough bark, and make a wish. None of the wishes ever came true, that she could remember, but that hadn't stopped her from wishing. She'd kept every leaf and feather that came down to her from its branches as a gift, as a promise that her life would get better. Someday the enchanted tree would come to her aid.

She was in no hurry to return to the old house on the street called Back Walls. Her mother's prescription had been a welcome excuse for a walk to the drugstore—no, the chemist. She was back in England now.

The ancient town of Stow-on-the-Wold on its high hill was lovely, gilded by the late afternoon sun.

But her life there was misery—misery in her childhood and fresh misery now. She shivered again in the icy breeze, which carried a faint but very foul stench—someone's bad drains, she supposed. There was no magic in her life these days.

Cecily looked up at a flash of black and white to see a pair of magpies alight side by side on a branch above her head. A half-forgotten childhood rhyme came into her head. "One for sorrow, two for joy," she murmured. She had no lack of sorrow. Joy would make a change—and with the thought, a purple and black feather spiraled down to kiss her outstretched palm.

Cecily said, "Thank you," aloud, and tucked the feather into a pocket. Magpies were mostly considered unlucky in English superstition, but she'd always liked them, and Native American people said carrying a magpie's feather brought courage and good luck.

A surge of unreasoning hope warmed Cecily, in spite of the chill in the air. She could use some good luck for a change, and above all, she needed courage.

A wave of harsh sound swamped her when she let herself into the house, as if her key in the front door turned the crank of a perverse music box. Her mother's bitter voice demanded, "Have you been to China and back? You've been gone long enough."

Her thirteen-year-old son Drew's simultaneous complaint—"Why didn't you tell me you were going to the drugstore?"— began as a baritone grumble, broke in the middle, and ended, to his visible fury, in a soprano whine. "You *knew* I wanted a soda!"

If Cecily had ever spoken to her mother that way, she would have called down a rain of angry words upon her head, and been sent to her room without supper. But although her mother still cursed Cecily with every other breath, she never scolded Drew.

This had surprised Cecily at first, but her mother was a realist. Though she relished inducing helpless misery in Cecily several times a day, she'd apparently recognized that Drew's egotism made him immune to all her self-pity, sarcasm, and rage. Now she ignored him as usual, and went on with her own complaint.

"What in bloody hell were you were thinking, you stupid little bitch, staying out so long? You know perfectly well I always have supper at quarter past five. Regular meals are important to my health! Are you trying to ruin my digestion?"

"Don't worry, Mother, your supper will be ready on time. It's only 4:30. It won't take me forty-five minutes to cook scrambled eggs and toast."

"Scrambled eggs?" Her tone of outrage was appropriate to an offer of pig slop. "I don't want scrambled eggs. That's baby food! I'll have a grilled chicken breast, with buttered asparagus."

"Unfortunately, we have neither chicken nor asparagus in the house. When I asked what you wanted for supper, you said you only wanted scrambled eggs, so there was no need to shop. I'll go back out now if you give me the money, but supper will be a bit late."

"What do you mean, give you money? I just gave you money an hour ago."

"You gave me the exact cost of your medicine. There was no change." *As you very well know.* When the chemist had called to say her refill was ready, Cecily's mother had asked the price and doled out the exact amount to the penny.

"You can't bear to spend even a few measly pence on your poor old mother, is that it? And why should supper be late? The Tesco is only five minutes from here."

"Five minutes by car, Mother. It's twenty each way on foot." *I don't have a car, remember, and you take great pleasure in refusing to let me to drive yours.*

"Anyway, I'm out of money until payday."

As soon as the words left her mouth, Cecily knew she'd suffer all evening for that mistake. Her pay was a touchy subject with her mother.

Three months ago a hospital social worker had located Cecily in Cheltenham and told her that Laetitia Moreton, her mother, had suffered a series of strokes, adding apologetically, "She says not to bother visiting, though. She won't see you."

Two weeks ago another social worker had called, from a nursing home. Mrs. Moreton no longer required skilled nursing, and could go home, provided she had a live-in caregiver. To Cecily's astonishment, her mother wished to offer her the job.

Three months earlier Cecily would have turned her down flat. But, back in England after fourteen years in America as a housewife, her lack of work history had made it impossible to get a job with decent pay, and her meager savings were nearly gone.

After long, painful thought, Cecily accepted the job, on condition she was hired and paid through an agency. Cecily knew better to put herself in her mother's financial power.

Throughout Cecily's childhood, her mother had manipulated her allowance. She'd withhold a portion for unspecified "infractions," or claim Cecily hadn't done all her chores, or give her only half, promising the rest later, then accuse Cecily of lying when she asked for it. In the end Cecily's father paid her allowance himself, though it was meant to come from the housekeeping budget. He'd learned to choose his battles.

Clearly her mother had looked forward to playing games with Cecily's wages. In the two weeks since Cecily's arrival, she'd already treated her to five outraged rants on her lack of family feeling.

Cecily closed her ears to a fresh spate of abuse as she fetched a glass of water, opened the medicine bottle and shook out a pill. She wondered how much more she could take before she quit—if her mother didn't fire her first. She watched dispassionately as her mother broke off in the middle of a sentence to swallow her pill and then opened her mouth to spout more rage and profanity. She watched Drew's jaw drop at his grandmother's foul-mouthed invective, which left even his father's bad language behind. Clearly, against his will, he was impressed.

Abruptly Cecily turned and left the room, followed by her mother's furious shouts. She set the glass beside the kitchen sink, feeling as though a wall of thicker glass separated her from the world, and set about preparing her mother's supper. After a time she vaguely noticed that the bellows of rage from the front room had trailed off, and enjoyed the quiet.

Drew ended the brief peace, joining her in the kitchen to voice his grievances. "Mom! Why did we have to move to this stupid place? All my friends are in Seattle, my school and everything. Why couldn't we stay there?"

"You know why we're here. We can't live on what your father pays in child support—*when* he pays.

I couldn't find work in Seattle, or Cheltenham. This is the only job I could get."

"But why do we have to live with this… this *witch*?"

Cecily wisely ignored his description of his grandmother. "Part of the job. We won't be here forever. I'm saving for our own place. Would you rather be in a shelter?"

"Everything sucks since you left Dad! All my friends are far away. We had a nice house and stuff. I know you and Dad didn't get along too well, but so what? Everyone's parents fight. You didn't have to *leave*."

"I had my reasons." Drew's petulant face blurred into the face of his father. Shaking off the vision, she was grateful that Drew had her blue eyes.

She couldn't have borne the daily sight of his father's dark eyes in her son's face.

"What reasons? You could have stayed if you wanted to, but you're too selfish. Now you've ruined my whole life, you stupid bitch!"

Cecily froze in shock, staring at him.

She'd put up with a lot from Drew. She knew he missed his friends, and she understood that to a boy raised in Seattle, a quaint English town like Stow might as well be Outer Mongolia. But before he had his grandmother's example, he'd never spoken to her that way.

"That's enough," Cecily said sharply. Her commanding tone surprised them both. "You will apologize to me, and then you will leave this room."

Drew blushed scarlet with shame and lowered his eyes. "Sorry," he muttered, and almost ran from the kitchen.

Cecily watched him go, her body shaking with a rush of adrenaline. He'd shocked himself too, she thought. The ding of the toaster brought her back to her tasks, but as she dished up scrambled eggs and buttered toast, she wondered where she'd found that voice of authority. Maybe the Native Americans were right about magpie feathers.

The tray she took to her mother reflected Cecily's high standards, not any affection for the old harridan. On an embroidered linen cloth sat a gold-edged china plate of crisp toast and perfect scrambled eggs. A small silver bowl held preserves, another held the imported chutney that was her mother's preferred condiment, and cut glass salt and pepper shakers flanked a stalk of sky-blue hyacinth in a crystal bud vase.

"I told you I did not want scrambled eggs!" Her mother glared at Cecily, and waited for her to stammer an apology. "Well? What do you have to say for yourself?"

Cecily looked at her without expression. "Nothing," she answered.

At Cecily's response, her mother's face grew purple, and she gobbled and snorted with incoherent rage. With sudden violence, she flung the whole tray to the floor.

Cecily glanced at the mess, then turned without a word and left the room.

Chapter Two

Cecily sat in the tree's lap and leaned against the trunk. She felt no agitation, only a flat empty calm. Gradually her breath and heartbeat slackened, and as the warmth of exertion from her brisk walk wore off, she grew cold. She hadn't stopped for a jacket.

Time seemed to grow fluid, expanding and contracting, looping back on itself. Sitting in the tree's lap, she was six again instead of thirty-six, and then sixteen, seeking comfort for the loss of her father to a slow cancer.

After her father died, Cecily had stayed only to finish school, and fled to Cheltenham the day after graduation. She had no friends to miss, thanks to her mother's ban on associating with the "lower orders"—meaning all her schoolmates.

Amazed at her own daring, she'd found herself a bed-sit, and a job in a tea shop where not even the rudest customers dared to behave in public as her mother behaved in private.

Poverty, never-ending aches in her back and feet, even the noise and dirt of the city, were paradise at first in comparison to life with her mother, especially the last two years. But all the same, those things had been hard on a girl who'd grown up in the timeless beauty of Stow.

One day a handsome American came along, to chat her up in the tea shop and then take her out to dinner. In the sun of his attention, Cecily blossomed. A month later he married her and took her to Seattle.

She'd been humbly grateful, she remembered with a shiver, ashamed of how little she had to offer him. Later she'd understood that her dowry was her naïve willingness to put herself in his power, in a distant land where she had not even the protection of citizenship. He'd chosen her precisely for her timidity, for her lack of family or friends to defend her.

Cecily wrenched her thoughts away from the horror of her years in America. Once the divorce was final, and Drew's father had scornfully waived his visitation rights, she'd returned to England. She'd longed to stop being a foreigner, and foolishly imagined that she'd find work in her native country … Another miserable and futile train of thought.

She couldn't keep living like this, caught between the endless demands of mother and son, further diminished every moment by their disrespect. She didn't try to think of places to run to, or of ways to die; she just knew she couldn't go on this way any longer.

She spoke aloud, softly. "Tree, if there is any magic in you at all, help me now."

The air grew colder, darkened to deep violet-blue, as she sat in the lap of the enchanted tree waiting for something to change. Streetlights came on, pale gold in the twilight. A raucous cloud of magpies swept into the tree's branches.

Automatically Cecily counted them... eight, nine... ten. The tenth settled on a low branch only a few feet above her head, something bright dangling from its beak. The object caught the light of the streetlamp, and flared with sudden crimson fire.

As she stared in wonder, a ferocious gust of wind hit her, slamming her back against the tree's trunk. Without thinking, Cecily reached out and the magpie swooped down to drop its treasure directly into her cupped hands: a ruby pendant on a silver chain.

Cecily slipped the chain over her head and dropped the ruby down the neck of her jersey—none too soon. Another burst of wind shrieked around her like an invisible demon, plucking with icy fingers at the silver chain. The indescribably foul stench of its breath made her gasp and retch, but the wind's efforts were to no avail. Where the stone rested on her skin, she felt a comforting warmth, and a soft red light shone like a lamp through the fabric of her jersey.

As abruptly as it had arrived, the wind departed, with one last fading shriek. All the magpies rose up in a whirl of black and white, with sudden gleams of blue, and flew away.

Cecily got unsteadily to her feet, wondering if she'd imagined it all, but a trace of the wind's foulness lingered in the air, and inside her jersey, below the base of her throat, the ruby pulsed with a warm steady light.

She'd always known the tree was magic.

Cecily turned to face it, and gasped in astonishment. Faint at first, but growing stronger as she watched, narrow bands of light outlined the shape of a door in the bark.

The door looked incredibly old. Its carved panels depicted a forest of intertwining branches, with deer and foxes and owls peering from gaps in the foliage. A knocker took shape, of corroded bronze turquoise with verdigris, in the form of a male face with hair and beard of leafy vines. She recognized the Green Man, ancient symbol of Nature's unstoppable powers of death and rebirth.

Cecily stared into eyes that were suddenly alive, regarding her with indifferent awareness tinged with mockery. The Green Man seemed to dare her to lift the ring in his mouth and knock.

Who would answer if she did? What unimaginable dangers lay beyond that door?

Even in her deepest despair, Cecily had always been too stubborn to consider ending her life. But... to risk it? When there was so little joy or peace in it, why not try for something new?

With trembling fingers she lifted the bronze ring and let it fall—once, twice, three times. The dull clang of metal against wood sounded frighteningly loud in the evening stillness, and with each clang the echoes grew louder, multiplied into a cacophony... The cloud of magpies returned to perch in the treetop, calling out to her in their harsh voices.

The door swung open. No one—*no one visible*—stood inside. Cecily saw only trees, a grove of oaks as ancient as *her* tree. Morning sunlight fell golden on their trunks, their broad branches, their summer foliage.

As she stood marveling, the wind came roaring back, assaulting her with its horrid stench. Cecily felt a push on her back like two strong hands shoving her forward. She stumbled over the threshold—and heard the door slam shut behind her.

Chapter Three

Cecily stood on a high green hill, bare of trees except for the circle of majestic oaks before her. Sunshine lay warm on her back and shoulders. A wild sweet scent arose from tiny white flowers in the springy turf beneath her feet, and the song of a meadowlark spiraled up to the cloudless blue sky.

To either side, the land fell away in wave after wave of forested hills that made her think of the furred flanks of giant beasts. To her right the forest ended at the base of low purple mountains; a distant sparkle to her left might be the sea.

Cecily turned and saw no sign of the door by which she'd entered, only the same flowery turf sloping away, the same low forest-clad hills. In dream-like calm, she turned and walked toward the grove.

A tingle ran through her as she stepped between two massive tree trunks, as though she'd crossed an electrified barrier. The air in the grove quivered with an energy she could almost see.

The landscape surrounding the hill seemed timeless, but the grove— The grove was something else. The circle of ancient oaks enclosed a space that seemed older than Time itself, newer than her next breath, like an incredibly ancient temple still in daily use.

By whom?

The trees' shade was a cool green twilight, but the center of the grove lay in bright sun. Suddenly too hot, Cecily pulled off her jersey and tied it around her waist. The ruby, unveiled, gleamed in the sun above the low neck of her tee shirt.

A boulder occupied the center of the clear space at the grove's heart, a great pale gray rock veined with rusty dark red...

The ruby's light flared up, making her blink. When she opened her eyes, she saw not a rock but an altar, a stone slab, as wide as she was tall and twice as long, carved around the edge with deeply-cut runes. The clotted streaks down its sides must be dried blood.

Cecily blinked again.

She stared at the altar, willing it to be innocent rock, but no matter how hard she squinted, she couldn't make the altar vanish. She realized the boulder was only a veil of illusion laid over the bloodstained altar.

Even in the hot sun, Cecily shivered. She hoped it was animals' blood spilled there, but she'd read once that the Druids had practiced human sacrifice. Was this a Druids' grove?

Cecily looked around the circle of mighty trees, and then down at the ruby, wondering what was real, what was illusion.

A wren sat on a branch peering at her. Cecily didn't like its beady-eyed stare, but when she held up the ruby, the bird was still a bird.

When a mottled brown hare leaped into the clearing, though, the ruby lit up again. The creature stopped, hopped up onto the altar and stared at her, and through the misty outline of the long-eared beast,

Cecily saw a tiny old woman, her face both clever and cruel. She'd heard old tales of witches who traveled in the form of hares. In this land, it appeared, legends were truth.

To Cecily's relief, the creature, after a long look at her, left the clearing with one bound, disappearing into the shadows under the trees.

Cecily wanted no more of the grove. She crossed the open space quickly, giving the altar a wide berth, and ducked under the trees again. Her straining eyes made out a gleam of daylight ahead, and soon she'd left the green darkness for the light of day.

She emerged from the grove and saw the land falling away into forested lowland, as on the hill's other sides—with one difference. A broad road, paved with closely fitted blocks of stone, began at her feet and divided the dark forest ahead. Her eyes followed the pale ribbon until it vanished over a rise, and then her feet too began to follow. She wondered where the road led, but it didn't matter. She didn't know where she was going anyway.

Cecily was very much aware of the teeming life of the forest to either side, and glad of the sunny open width of the road between the stretches of dark woods. Red deer peered at her between the branches of oaks and elms clad in dusty summer foliage. Blackbirds chirped and twittered. Squirrels scolded from thickets of glossy dark holly studded with blood-red berries. Occasionally foxes looked up from the undergrowth. Once she saw a striped badger. Four magpies emerged from the wood and flew ahead of her down the road.

As the sun rose higher, she grew very thirsty, though not hungry. She felt no uneasiness, and yet somehow she didn't want to leave the road to search for a stream.

"Fair day to you, Lady."

Cecily whirled around at the man's voice, so fast she made herself dizzy—and saw no one. She turned slowly in a complete circle, and still didn't see the man who'd spoken.

"I mean you no harm," continued the deep pleasant voice. It seemed to come from the woods to her right. "Please do not fear me."

A huge black horse, powerful muscles rippling under its sleek hide, emerged from the shadows. It was enchantingly beautiful—and somehow terrifying. Hot yellow eyes met hers...

Then the ruby flared and pulsed against her skin, and she saw that the horse was a man.

"I'm not afraid," she said. The double vision made her dizzy for a moment, but as the image of the horse faded, she saw only the man beside her, tall and muscular, with thick golden brown hair like summer wheat above tanned skin and blue eyes. Something was familiar about him, but she couldn't place him.

"Fair day to you too," she added politely, "and it is a lovely one, isn't it? Where I came from, it's cold blustery March, but it seems to be Midsummer here."

"It's always Midsummer here," said the stranger, with a sigh. "You might get tired of it if you stay long enough."

"I don't plan to stay very long," she said. "How long have you been here?"

"Two weeks, or fourteen years. It depends on how you calculate it. I was very young when I came here."

"But… You must be as old as I am, or nearly." He could be a few years younger than her, but he had to be at least thirty.

"You see the man, then, not the horse?" he asked, in some surprise.

Cecily nodded. "It's this ruby." She held it up to show him, and saw his eyes widen. "It seems to cut through illusions. It showed me a little old witch disguised as a hare, and a bloodstained altar where I first saw only a rock."

"A powerful charm!" he exclaimed. "Guard it well. As for my appearance, fourteen years ago a Kerrighan stole me from the riverbank where I was fishing, and replaced me with a changeling of her own people. I've only been a horse for seven years, since I declined to marry one of Queen Maeve's ladies in waiting. The Queen said that if I did not choose to ride her lady, then her lady should ride me."

When Cecily blinked in astonishment at the crudity of the Queen's remark, he added, "The folk here are... plain-spoken."

"What is this place?" Cecily cried. "What is a Kerrighan, and who is Queen Maeve? Oh, wait, I know who Maeve is, the queen of the fairies in Celtic mythology. But how...? But why?" Her long day, already drawing toward its close before she'd stumbled into this new day, caught up with her all at once. "I don't understand."

She reeled with exhaustion, and found herself leaning against a warm shoulder—or was it the flank of a horse?

"You are very tired, my lady. Will you not sit down for a moment?"

"I am tired," she agreed shakily, "and so very thirsty."

"Can you walk just a little farther? I'll lead you to a stream."

Cecily nodded. *Why should I trust him?* she wondered. *He might be planning to rape me or murder me, or just lose me in the deep* woods. With a hysterical urge to giggle, she thought, *And I don't even have any breadcrumbs to drop.* But she didn't see why he'd want to do any of those things.

Ruby, she thought, as she wavered to her feet, *don't you have any advice for me?*

Nothing happened. The ruby did not flare up in warning as it had in the grove. But its warmth where it lay against her flesh was comforting.

Even if she didn't trust him—and how could she ever trust any man again?—she really had no choice. Now that she'd acknowledged her thirst, it was a torment that drove all other considerations away. She followed him wordlessly along a narrow track through the woods.

Chapter Four

Cecily sat on a mossy log at the edge of a sunlit clearing—not a grove, to her relief, just an open place where a tree had fallen long ago. She had drunk her fill of sweet water from a stream that meandered across the clearing, and was now content to rest.

Looking at her companion, she admitted to herself that his presence was a comfort. He wasn't exactly handsome, but he looked intelligent and good-natured, like a big friendly dog.

"Are you hungry at all?" he asked.

"Ravenous!" She hadn't known it until he spoke, and now she could think of nothing else. "Do you have any food?" She looked doubtfully at him. He had no bag, and the pockets of his close-fitting jeans were obviously empty. The only bulge was— Cecily blushed and looked away. *I'm as ignorant of men as any child could be*, she thought. Her ex-husband was a monster, not a man, and she had been with no other.

"I have no food—yet," he said. "But even in this form, I still have some of the privileges of this realm." He collected dry twigs and heaped them on a flat stone as he spoke, so awkwardly that Cecily realized that he could only move as a horse did. Then he stared fixedly at the wood, his eyes suddenly no longer blue but a hot yellow, and soon a tongue of flame arose from the center of the pile of sticks.

"If you'll keep this going," he said when the fire had taken hold, "I'll catch some fish."

Cecily obediently gathered wood and fed the fire, pausing to watch and grin a little at the comic spectacle of her new friend fishing. His antics—stomping his feet in the shallow water and kicking fish up onto the mossy bank—reminded her that his present form was not human.

When he'd flung three small fish out of the stream, he killed them cleanly with a sharp kick to each head. "I'm sorry, I'm afraid you must deal with them now."

"No worries." With no knife she couldn't gut the trout, so she impaled them on green twigs and propped them up by the fire. She'd had enough Japanese food out west not to mind raw fish, and began to nibble the first when it was barely singed. Nothing had ever tasted better.

Her companion, meanwhile, bent his head to graze—a ludicrous spectacle that made Cecily choke back a giggle.

He turned to look at her with an expression of innocent inquiry, and Cecily was lost. She laughed aloud, and at his answering grin, she went off into gales of uncontrollable mirth.

"I'm sorry," she said, when she could speak, "I know you're in the body of a horse, but that's not what I see, and... and, I can't help it! You have no idea how funny you look grazing."

"No, but I can imagine," he said sympathetically, and laughed too.

That set Cecily off again, but when the last gasping giggle had abated, her mind returned to her questions. "Please, tell me, what is this place?" Innate courtesy made her add, "My name is Cecily, by the way, Cecily Moreton." She'd reclaimed her maiden name in the divorce.

"Cecily," he cried, "How wonderful to see you. I can't imagine why I didn't cecognize you. Do you remember me, Dane Blacksmith? I was in love with you all the years we were in school together, I swear." His eyes said his feelings hadn't changed much.

"I do remember you," she replied shyly. "I think I was in love with you too—but my mother made sure we never spoke to each other outside the classroom."

"Yes, she was always there to whisk you away as soon as the bell rang."

"She would have sent me away to preserve me from lower-class acquaintance, but my father insisted I go to the local school. But, Dane... why did those people steal you and bring you here—the Kerrighans, you said?"

He stared into the embers of the fire. "I've had plenty of time to think about it, and I believe they took me because I *am* a blacksmith, like my father before me, and his father before him—back to the dawn of time, to hear my grandda tell it. We don't shoe as many horses as we used to, let alone forging swords or plowshares, but we do a very nice line in wrought iron garden gates and ornamental hinges."

"I don't understand," said Cecily.

"My substitute is a poor smith, and the business is failing in his hands—which is the point: one less skilled smith in the world. The Folk don't care much for cold iron. Their own weapons are all of bronze."

At Cecily's bewildered look, he laughed. "I'm sorry, you need explanations, not more confusion. What is this place?" he echoed. "It has many names. One of them is Faerie. As far as I can tell, it is Britain in the time of the old gods, before the coming of humankind. To the modern mind Maeve is the Queen of the Fairies, but here she is much more. She's the most powerful of our land's ancient gods, as capricious as she is mighty, easily roused to anger and greatly to be feared. I still don't know how I dared to refuse the marriage she planned for me."

He sighed. "Well, that's not true: I do know. I've seen what happens to a human that's mated to one of the Folk."

"*What* happens? And what is a Kerrighan?" asked Cecily.

"Love, as the Folk know it, is no more than sexual infatuation. When the Folk take human lovers or mates, they use them up. They suck them dry of all energy and hope, and then spit them out. What's left of the person afterward doesn't usually live very long. Do you remember *La Belle Dame sans Merci*? 'Alone and palely loitering.' Keats got it right."

Cecily shivered. That sounded too much like her own marriage, though there'd been nothing otherworldly about her mate. She repeated, "What are Kerrighans?"

"The original Druids. They're not human, you know. They're a race of minor gods who tend the sacred groves. Human Druids came later. The Kerrighans only used men as sacrificial victims at first but later they took human disciples and taught them the worship of the groves."

Usually Cecily loved history and mythology, but they didn't interest her at the moment. "Have you really been here so long?"

"Yes and no. Time moves oddly here. I've been here two weeks by the Folk's reckoning, and sometimes it feels like no more than that. But I've aged at the same rate as the changeling in my place, so I've lived fourteen human years here—and sometimes it feels like no less."

"So the stories are true, and if I stay here for six months, I'll go home and find that everyone I knew is dead?" It shocked her how little that idea bothered her. She had to remind herself that she did love her son: he was just going through a difficult stage. But she couldn't say the same for her mother.

"Not exactly," he said. "That's only if you eat the Folk's food. The old tales about goblin fruit are true. But the fish you ate were just fish, untouched by magic."

"Thanks," said Cecily. "That's reassuring—or it would be, if I had anything to go back to," she added bitterly. "My mother hates me, and my son has no respect for me."

"How old is he?" Dane asked. "If he's in his teens, he has no respect for anyone. Kids that age hate everybody, especially their mothers."

Cecily made no reply, as a raucous cloud of magpies flew into the clearing. Most of them flew away, but three birds remained to perch all in a row on a branch, and four more perched on another branch. They regarded her and Dane in silence, with their heads on one side.

"Three for a girl and four for a boy," Cecily murmured. "That's me and you in our schooldays, I guess. Is there any way to get you home again?" she wondered aloud.

"That I cannot tell you. I suspect the Kerrighans' claim to me can only be overruled by the Queen herself, and she's not pleased with me just now."

As suddenly as they'd come, the magpies departed. The sky overhead darkened with stormclouds, and a gust of malodorous wind lashed the nearby trees.

"Oh, it's that horrible wind again!" Cecily cried. "Where does it come from? It smells like scorched and rotting meat."

"That's the Kerrighans' wind. It carries the odor of their burnt sacrifices. You've smelled it before?" Dane seemed startled.

"Yes, just before I came here. The wind tried to snatch the ruby from me, and then it pushed me through the door in the tree."

"But that's—" Whatever Dane meant to say, he broke off, as a huge raven flapped into the clearing like a piece of darkness come loose from the night. The bird fixed its yellow eyes on Dane and spoke.

The harsh syllables were incomprehensible to Cecily, but they clearly had some meaning Dane could follow. Cecily held up the ruby, but the bird's appearance didn't change. More than a common bird it might be, but it wasn't something else in disguise. With one last croak, the creature departed.

"Cecily, we're in danger," Dane said. "Even though they pushed you through the door themselves, you being here with the ruby alarms the Kerrighans.

Now that you and I have met, I think they fear you'll help me escape—though I don't see how. So they've set the Questing Beast to pursue us. If it should catch us, I fear for our lives."

"Oh, what is it?" Cecily wanted to laugh again. "It sounds ridiculous, but horrible!"

"It is all that: an ugly hodgepodge of many different animals, and the worst parts of each. Some of it's bristly, and some is slimy, and it makes a noise like an entire pack of hunting dogs."

He paused and held his breath for a moment. "Do you hear it?"

With horror, Cecily realized she did: a confused clamor, like dozens of dogs baying and barking all at once—for blood.

"It's too close for you to flee on foot," Dane said. "You'll have to ride me."

Cecily looked at Dane in surprise. In spite of her laughter at the sight of him grazing, she'd forgotten the enchantment again. She'd only *seen* him as a horse for a brief moment before the ruby showed her the man. Now, try as she might, she could only see his human face. "I'll have to take off the ruby to see you as a horse," she said hesitantly.

"No, don't do that," Dane replied. "We need your abilities, and the ruby helps you focus them."

"You're right, we need all the help the ruby can give us. But I don't think it's anything to do with me," she said, though his words warmed her heart. "I don't have any special powers without the ruby."

"Why do you doubt yourself, Cecily? I know something of the rubies—this is one of several—and, as powerful as they are, they cannot create new talents in their wearers. They only awaken or strengthen the talents the wearer already possesses. The gift of the True Sight, that comes from within you."

"If you say so," she muttered, disbelieving.

"My dear," he said urgently, "we have no time for discussion. Close your eyes, and see if your sense of touch tells you I'm in the shape of a horse." He positioned himself beside a large boulder—it really was a boulder, Cecily saw thankfully—and said, "Step up on this, and you should be able to get onto my back."

Cecily stood on the boulder beside Dane. When she looked at him, the top of his head came up to her chin, but when she obediently closed her eyes and reached out to touch him, her hand encountered the broad back of a horse. Giving herself no time to think, she grasped the invisible mane with both hands and heaved herself up.

"I hope I don't fall off," she said doubtfully. "I've never ridden."

"You can't fall off. I'm a pooka."

"Pookas—I've heard of them, I think. Fairy horses. Aren't they evil?"

"Like so many things here, yes, they are, or at least amoral—but *I'm* not. I'm only in the shape of one. All the same, I do have the pooka's ability to hold its rider fast—so you can't fall off me until I release you. Ready?"

Cecily took a deep breath and tightened her grip on the mane. "Ready."

With one terrifying, exhilarating leap, they were off.

Chapter Five

Cecily leaned against Dane's comforting solidity and closed her eyes. The earth seemed to rock and heave under her feet, and her knees kept trying to buckle. She rested one arm on the horse's sweat-dampened back, and felt powerful muscles ripple as his sides heaved with gasping breaths. They'd careened through the forest faster than she'd thought any racehorse could go.

Cecily too was gasping and sweating, though all she'd done was hang on for dear life and dodge the trees' lower branches.

"I believe we've outrun the Questing Beast." Dane seemed to be regaining his breath.

His voice, as much as his words, put new courage into her. She'd come to rely on his help, and by now she—*almost*—trusted him. Laughter had helped, she thought. Her ex-husband had never in his life laughed in honest mirth. She'd learned to recognize his cruel little smile as a warning of some new horror he'd planned. She shivered, and wrenched her mind back to the present—or whatever time this was. At least it was a time in which she was free of *him*.

"Yes, thanks to you," she said. "I can't hear it any more. And I did not fall off."

Of course, she couldn't have fallen off if she'd tried. No one could dismount from a pooka without its permission, which most of them weren't inclined to give.

The demon horses of Celtic lore were so beautiful that to see one was to desire to ride it. But once mounted on a pooka's back, the unwary human was held fast by some magic in the beast's hide, until the terrifying headlong gallop ended with a plunge into the depths of a lake, and the rider drowned. Luckily Cecily had been in no danger of drowning by this pooka.

At the raucous cries of a flock of magpies overhead, Cecily opened her eyes, and once again the difference between what she saw and what she felt made her dizzy. Although she *felt* that her arm was draped over the back of a horse, she *saw* that it was slung around the shoulders of a tall, broad-shouldered man—a stranger, and yet a man in whose face she caught occasional glimpses of the blue-eyed boy she'd once longed to know better.

"Magpies are amazing birds, aren't they?" Dane's conversational tone helped to calm her unease. He must have sensed her agitation.

"They have a bad reputation in England," Cecily replied, "but I always liked them as a child, and in America they're supposed to bring good luck."

"I agree with the Americans, then," Dane said, "and with you. Do you know the collective noun for them, like a murder of crows or a parliament of owls?"

"A conventicle, or a tidings." Cecily fought the urge to giggle hysterically. *How very English we are.* They stood in a weird, incalculably ancient land, in mortal danger, chattering—*like magpies?*—about trivialities. She almost expected to find a porcelain teacup in her hand.

"A conventicle is a dissenting church. Maybe the black and white reminded people of Quakers or Puritans. But I like 'tidings' better—they do seem to bring messages, don't they? Magpies and their cousins the ravens."

"Like the raven who told you about the Beast. How were you able to understand him?"

"I've been here long enough to pick up several languages. I can speak some Owl, and quite a lot of Robin. I know a little Selkie, too, but for some reason the bird languages come easier to me—maybe because my mother has always talked to birds. Her last name is even Byrd, Byrd-Blacksmith. Anyway, the ravens love to talk. They don't take sides here;

they just carry gossip back and forth, and watch what happens."

"But you don't know any magpie speech?"

"No. I've never seen magpies here before. You must have brought them with you."

"Dane," Cecily spoke hesitantly. "Why do you think the ruby came to me?"

"How did it come to you? I don't think you ever told me."

"A magpie dropped it into my hands," she said. "That's what made me think of it."

"And then you came through the door into this country—and I met you."

Dane's voice dropped on those last words, taking on a serious tone, and a warmth that made Cecily's heart beat a little faster.

Embarrassed, she hastened into speech. "Please tell me what you know of this ruby. You said earlier that it's one of several."

"Yes, it's a fragment of a gem that once belonged to Queen Maeve. Each piece brings great power for good or for evil: not in itself, but by aiding its wearer's own dormant talents. One wearer might develop healing powers; another might learn to communicate across great distance. In you it has awakened the ability to see through disguises."

"Too bad the gift wasn't awakened fourteen years ago, then," she said bitterly. "It would have saved me from marrying a monster."

"Cecily, I am so sorry."

To her surprise, Cecily did not resent his sympathy—maybe because his words were so simple, spoken so calmly and yet in such a warm voice, that she believed he really did care that she had been made unhappy.

Suddenly embarrassed, she realized her arm was still draped across his shoulders, and she removed it. "I've never told anyone about what happened to me. It's too horrible to talk about."

"But you should talk about it," he said seriously. "That's an important part of healing. I don't mean you should tell *me*; you don't know me—though I'd be honored to hear anything you want to say. But for your own sake, do tell someone. My mother always taught me to do that, when I had nightmares. She said the only way to keep them from haunting me was to talk about them, and I believe that's just as true of bad experiences."

Cecily knew it was good advice, though she didn't see herself following it any time soon. "Your mother sounds like a wise woman."

"She is, literally. She belongs to a Circle in Stow, the People of the Craft. She never told me much about what they do, but I believe the Circle has held the line against evil in the town and the surrounding villages for centuries. Now that I know about the rubies, I wouldn't be surprised if some of those women and men also wear them."

"Maybe even your mother."

"Maybe so."

"I wonder, though: why hasn't she come to rescue you?"

"She may not realize that I'm truly gone. So many parents in our time have their hearts broken by seeing a beloved child turn into a stranger overnight, from drugs or mental illness."

"I know exactly what you mean, and it's one of my greatest terrors. My son is thirteen now, and I can't help watching every bad habit in him to see if it becomes something worse." Cecily shook her head to clear it of such ideas. She had enough to worry about here and now.

"Yes, and knowing all that, and maybe not being gifted like you with the True Sight, she may doubt the truth of her sense that my replacement is not her son."

A new and more pleasant thought struck Cecily.

"But maybe she does know. Maybe the Circle *is* trying to help you, by sending the magpies, and opening the door for me into this land. I came here from Stow too, you know."

"I can imagine my mother sending magpies, I'll give you that. I can't tell you how many times I've seen her face to face with a magpie, with her head on one side like she was listening, and then she'd answer."

"I'm glad the magpies are here. I don't see yet how I can help you, but there will be a way. I know there will be a way, because I have the ruby—and the magpies gave it to me."

"I believe you are right," Dane said. "But it's not just the ruby that will help us. Cecily, it's you, *you* wearing the ruby, focusing your inner power through it. Meeting you is the best thing that's ever happened to me in this strange land."

Cecily thought he exaggerated, but she couldn't help feeling a glow of pleasure at his words. "You're the best thing that's happened to me here too."

All at once the horrible wind was back, with all its foul stench, raging up and down the road, tearing the leaves off the trees, shrieking like a host of souls in torment.

Cecily turned involuntarily to hide her face against Dane's chest—and it *was* his chest, a man's chest clad in an ordinary Twenty-First Century tee-shirt, not any part of a horse.

"They've lifted the enchantment," said Dane. "I wonder why."

THE DOOR IN THE TREE

Chapter Six

"I wonder why," Dane repeated. "It can't be for any reason that's good for us."

Cecily drew back sharply, her cheeks flushed red. Though Dane had been human to her *sight* all along, knowing he was actually in animal form had somehow exempted him from her fear of men. Now that he was back in his true shape, embarrassment and distrust flooded her mind. *I rode on him*, she thought, and her blush deepened.

If Dane saw her distress, he ignored it. "Maybe the Kerrighans asked the Queen to undo the spell," he said gloomily. "They don't want us to have the pooka's speed, I'm guessing."

Cecily wrenched her mind back to their problems. "If the Kerrighans don't want me and the ruby here, why did their wind push me through the door?"

"Maybe they thought they could steal the ruby from you here more easily than in your own land."

"Well, they thought wrong. I won't give it up, and I won't give up on getting us out of here." Cecily surprised herself with her determined tone. "But what will they do to us next?"

"I don't know. I don't understand all the rules of this land. Maybe by bringing me here and replacing me with one of their own, they've made me a kind of citizen, whether they meant to or not. It feels that way, because I've been given all the Folk's everyday skills, water-finding and fire-starting and so on. If that's true, then they can't simply kill me. But they can imprison me. And you— I'm afraid of what they might do to you."

"But I— Dane, I have the ruby. I can feel it making me stronger and braver, the longer I wear it." As she spoke, the stone grew warm against her skin, and pulsed with a soft red glow.

"Instead of worrying about what they'll do next, maybe we should decide what *we'll* do next," she said.

"I don't really have any ideas right now." Dane ran his hands through his thick hair in a puzzled way, vividly reminding Cecily of their school days.

She chuckled at the vision, and Dane looked at her enquiringly. "Do you remember our teacher Mrs. Claremont?" she asked.

"Mrs. Churchmouse," he cried delightedly. "We called her that for the way she nibbled at her pencil with her little teeth. Whatever made you think of her?"

"The way you ruffled your hair just now. You always did that when she called on you."

"That was because I never knew the answer," he said ruefully. "I'm afraid I don't know the answer now, either."

Cecily liked his frankness. "How can I meet the Queen? Maybe I can just ask her to release you."

"I can take you to the Queen easily enough, but what then? However well you conceal the ruby, she'll sense it and try to take it from you. For this much I know: she's trying to get all the rubies back, and if she gets even half of them, she'll have far greater reach into our time."

"What would she do then? What *could* she do?"

"She would enforce her worship as it was in the time of her greatest power. Effectively she'd send us all back thousands of years, to the bad old days when humans were no more than slaves or playthings—not only for her but for still older gods, even less human-like than she is."

Cecily shuddered. "That's a horrible thought. I've read about the Old Powers of the earth. They're faceless and cruel, most of them, demanding blood sacrifice, and giving nothing in return, not even safety. That's what the Kerrighans worship in the groves, isn't it?"

"Exactly," said Dane. "Bringing your ruby anywhere near Maeve seems like a bad idea."

"But I don't think she *can* take it from me." Cecily didn't know where her belief came from, but she trusted it. "It's bonded to me now. When the great ruby broke up, I think her bond to it must have broken too. Maybe she can sense the rubies, but she can't steal them if they're bonded to their wearers."

Dane watched with awe as her ruby pulsed with light again. "Your ruby confirms your words, it seems. Good enough. Let us go to the Queen's court and see what chances."

Suddenly a tidings of magpies swooped from above to circle them. Cecily counted five—no, six, as they settled on the pavement of the road. The fifth, to her astonishment, strutted right up to her feet and stood staring up at her with its bright black eyes, while the last came to Dane.

"Aveta!" it cried.

Was it a name? A word in some foreign language? It was no ordinary bird call, and Cecily marveled that a bird's throat could form the human-sounding syllables.

"Aveta!" Dane echoed, astonished.

"What does it mean?"

"Aveta is a goddess of this land, and I think we are being told to visit her grove."

"Another grove?" Cecily shuddered with disgust.

"A very different grove, I promise you. Aveta is a goddess of life, not death."

"Okay, sure," she told Dane. "But why?"

"I'm only guessing, but it might be because she created the ruby in the first place. Let's get going, and I'll tell you the story as we walk." Dane led the way into a broad path like a green tunnel, worn deep into the earth and roofed with intertwined branches.

"Aveta is one of the Old Powers. There are some good ones, you know, besides the evil ones like Arawn, and the neutral ones like the Horned God Cernunnus. Compared to them, Maeve and her people are mere newcomers. Aveta's special care is for pregnant women."

Cecily's heart clenched in a pang of grief for the embryonic daughter she'd carried so briefly. Her ex-husband hadn't wanted a girl, and he'd done things to her that caused her to miscarry. Not that he'd ever shown much interest in his son, possibly because

Drew looked too much like her and not enough like him. She wrenched her mind back to Dane's words.

"Women who cannot conceive or who have difficult pregnancies come to bathe in her sacred spring. Long ago, a knight brought his sister to Aveta's grove. All their family had perished in a plague, and she was near her time. The baby was born in the grove, mother and child both healthy. In gratitude, the knight brought gifts to Aveta's altar, and spread her worship among his fellow knights. Aveta smiled upon him, and appeared to him in human form. Piercing her finger with a silver knife he'd given her, she shed one drop of her blood and shaped it into a great ruby, telling him to give it to a woman with a heart as pure and loving as his own."

"How did Maeve get it, then, and how was it broken?"

"The stories, whispered for fear of Maeve's anger, all begin with her seeing Aveta create the ruby, and coveting it. She appeared to the knight as a lovely young girl and charmed him into giving him the ruby. The stories disagree on what came next. Some say the knight tried to take it back when he realized who she was. Others say the ruby would not go to Maeve, and burned her fingers, so she threw it away in rage. All agree that it was shattered, and that Maeve seeks to bring the pieces together again to feed her power."

Cecily didn't know much about Maeve, but she had the impression of a spoiled child, self-willed, greedy, and vengeful—and with vast magical powers. "That must not happen." She spoke with firm resolve, and her ruby flared crimson on her throat as if it agreed.

"We are here," Dane said.

The path had been climbing steeply for some time. Now it emerged into a sunlit meadow atop a high round hill, much like the hill where Cecily had entered this land. Again she saw a ring of oaks before her, some young and slender, some in their prime, and some ancient, bowed and twisted with years. But even from a distance, she felt a sense of welcome from this grove.

One young oak drew her especially. Something about the placement of the limbs looked familiar, the whorls of the bark that formed a kindly face…

She ran forward eagerly, crying out in delight, "My tree!"

Dane smiled. "Looks like you've found an old friend."

"I have. Growing up, this tree was my only friend. It's much younger here, but I swear it's the same one." She looked from her tree to her ruby, and said slowly, "The door I came through was in this tree."

As she spoke, she laid her hand on the tree. The sun-warmed bark had an almost animal heat to the touch. Suddenly she flung both arms around the tree and laid one cheek against the trunk, as she had in her childhood—and this time she sensed a vibration, like a sound just beyond the limits of hearing: something like a heartbeat.

"So that's why the Kerrighans' wind pushed you," Dane said. "To send you to their grove instead of this one."

"But I'm here now. Let's go in." Cecily's tree and another stood a meter apart, branches twined together overhead, forming a narrow arch. She heard the sound of trickling water ahead, and the sense of welcome pulsing from the center of the grove was almost tangible. Her ruby pulsed again in response. Confidently she led the way, leaving Dane to follow.

THE DOOR IN THE TREE

Chapter Seven

At the heart of the grove, a round pool of water reflected blue sky. Opposite the entrance, the sacred spring bubbled up in a waist-high stone basin, falling over the edge to fill the pool.

"Come in, my children." The soft voice was hardly any louder than the rustle of the oak leaves in the gentle breeze. "Come, eat and drink and take your rest here, for you both are weary, and great exertions lie ahead of you before you may rest again."

Cecily looked for the speaker, but saw no one. She walked around the right side of the pool toward the ferny basin, and saw the altar, a modest wooden table standing in the shade behind the basin. On the altar stood two moon-silver goblets, flanking a platter and a shallow bowl made of hammered gold. The platter held small bread rolls and chunks of soft cheese; the bowl was heaped with fruit: apples, peaches, plums, soft dark figs and bunches of purple grapes.

Cecily took a goblet, dipped it into the basin to fill it, and held it aloft. "My heartfelt gratitude to you, Aveta, Lady of the Grove."

"Be welcome here," came the rustling murmur. Cecily wondered suddenly if the Goddess dwelt in one of the trees. Remembering the heartbeat she'd felt in her tree, she wondered if all the trees of this grove were people of a sort. Her tree had always been a person to her.

Cecily and Dane obeyed their invisible hostess, feasting and quenching their thirst, and then reclining on the thick emerald moss that carpeted the grove.

Aveta spoke again. "You were meant to come here, my daughter. Your friend says truly that the Kerrighans' wind sent you wrong. Your instinct about the tree you love, that also is truth. She has always watched over you while you were near to her, comforting you as best she could. Your love for her made it possible for me to open a door to you."

She, thought Cecily. *The Goddess calls my tree "she."*

"Stand up, my daughter, and approach my table again. One thing I must do for your safety, without delay."

On the altar the remains of the food had vanished and the dishes shone clean and empty, but a tiny silver knife lay on the golden platter. Dane stood back watching.

"Take off your necklace and place it in the bowl," came the voice. "Then get water in a goblet and pour it over the ruby."

Cecily obeyed in silence.

"Look down at the place where the ruby lay on your chest."

A tiny red dot marked her skin, seven inches below the base of her throat, a little above the swell of her breasts.

"Now take the knife and pierce your skin in that spot."

Again Cecily obeyed. The cut barely stung, and only a tiny droplet of blood emerged.

Where a young oak had stood, a female figure materialized. Aveta faced Cecily across the altar, her shape misty at first, then becoming more solid. Shorter even than Cecily, the Goddess had olive skin, black hair and warm brown eyes. A loose gown of russet cloth, belted with a green vine, revealed more than it hid of her voluptuous form.

Yet, even without touching the ruby, Cecily could still see the oak—and then, in the same place, a doe with two spotted fawns peering out from behind her, then an apple tree heavy with fruit, a fair-haired woman suckling an infant, and last of all, a sheaf of wheat bound together with a vine bearing purple grapes. All of these, she realized, were the true shape of the Goddess.

Aveta took up the knife in one hand and delicately touched the point to one finger. A single drop of blood fell into the bowl where the ruby lay. The ruby pulsed with light and then disappeared as the water in the bowl darkened to the color of wine.

"Look within," said the Goddess, "both of you."

Dane came to stand beside Cecily as she stared into the bowl. The surface of the water became a window, and she saw an old woman, wasted by disease, propped up in bed in a paneled room that Cecily recognized with amazement as a bedroom in her mother's house. The windows, the carved panels, the fireplace, all were unmistakable. Even the furniture was the same; only the coverlet and draperies were different.

Beside the bed sat a young woman, her handsome face marred by a look of arrogance, a sour twist to the mouth. With shock, and a sense of inevitability, Cecily realized she was seeing her mother in youth, and *her* mother, Lavinia Purcell, the grandmother Cecily had never known.

The old woman took something from under her pillow, and held it to her cheek, a look of regret and uncertainty on her face. Soft red light seeped through the clenched fingers, and when the hand opened, Cecily, unsurprised, saw a ruby on a silver chain.

Eagerly, imperiously, the young Laetitia put out her hand—and a tidings of magpies, seven of them, flew in the open window to alight on the bed. As Laetitia grabbed for it in vain, the seventh magpie snatched up the ruby in its beak, and the birds departed as they had arrived, a whirling cloud of black and white, shot with sudden gleams of blue.

"Seven for a secret," Cecily murmured. "We'll never know why."

"I can guess," Dane said. "But now we know why it came to you."

The picture vanished, and as Dane and Cecily watched, another formed.

A group of women and men in modern clothes sat around a kitchen table. Some wore rubies like Cecily's, all ablaze with power.

"Cecily, this is the Circle I told you about," cried Dane, "the People of the Craft. The blonde woman in blue is my mother—and you were right, she has a ruby. On her right is Luna, and then Goldie, Ben, Elise, Edward, Anita, Roly, Jane, and Violet."

The Circle was a diverse group, full of contrasts: frail elderly Violet and tall pale-haired Elise, the strapping farmer Edward and Luna the aging hippie. Clearly they were holding some kind of meeting—or even, to judge by the beams of light the rubies emitted, working magic.

Dane's mother was a kind-looking woman in her late fifties, with bright eyes and a habit of tipping her head to one side as if listening to something others didn't hear. *She talks to birds,* Cecily remembered. *She must listen to them too.*

Now she saw them: nine magpies perched around the room, and the tenth on Dane's mother's shoulder. Luna opened a small leather bag painted all over with runes, and took out a ruby on a silver chain. All the other rubies flared up bright, and so did the new one. Dane's mother's lips moved as if she spoke, and the bird hopped from her shoulder onto the table to pick up the necklace in its beak.

"Now we know," Dane said. "The Circle did send the ruby to you—and it's truly yours, inherited from your grandmother."

All at once the wine-colored water spun into a tiny whirlpool, faster and faster—and was gone. The silver chain had become part of the bowl, a delicate inlay, while as for the ruby—

"It looks soft," Cecily said wonderingly, "as though juice would run out if I squeezed it."

"Pick it up," said Aveta, invisible again. "Hold it to the place you cut."

It *was* soft to the touch, more like a ripe wild strawberry than a gemstone. Cecily held it carefully between thumb and forefinger, touched it to the tiny bead of blood on her chest—and gasped. The ruby grew smaller and still softer, mixed with the drop of blood, and then slipped inside the cut. The edges of the cut immediately closed over it, leaving smooth skin with no trace of a wound. But where the ruby had formerly rested on its chain, a small hexagonal patch of skin was red—not rough or sore, but smooth and simply red, like a birthmark.

Outside the grove the Kerrighans' wind howled and screeched, but the sound seemed to come from very far away, and within the grove not a single leaf was troubled. The circle of oaks held peace like wine in a cup.

A sudden wave of exhaustion hit Cecily, making her stumble and catch hold of the altar table to keep from falling. She hoped it wasn't sacrilege, but she was too tired to care.

Dane put a steadying arm around her. "Cecily, you must sleep. We are safe here."

"It was already evening when I left my world," she said apologetically, "and I'm sure I've been here at least half of another day. Yes, thank you, I will sleep." She lay down on the dry moss, with her jersey for a pillow, and closed her eyes.

In her dream she was still in the grove, and Aveta in human form stood beside her.

"Not even Maeve herself can tear the ruby from you now," Aveta said. "If she killed you, the ruby would dissolve and flow away with your heart's blood. Although I do not leave my grove, Maeve knows that I have ways to make her feel my displeasure, and so she dares not harm you. The ruby will only leave you when you choose to pass it on to your daughter."

Another pang of sorrow struck Cecily for the child she had lost, and the Goddess knelt beside her and stroked Cecily's hair off her face. The gentle touch made Cecily want to weep. She hadn't known affection since her father's death.

Aveta spoke again. "I grieve with you for the lost child, but she could not have thrived in her time and place. You will bear another daughter to inherit your ruby, I promise you."

"I dare not marry again," cried Cecily in anguish and terror.

"My child, you have been sorely wounded in body and in spirit. But there are good men as well as evil men in the world. Never forget that."

Cecily's eyes followed as the Goddess directed a glance at Dane, and she saw that he sat quietly under a tree, watching over her slumber.

"Before I send you home," Aveta continued, "you shall bathe in my pool and be healed of your wounds. In time you will marry and bear another child, a daughter conceived in love, not in pain and terror; a daughter born into community as you were not. Now sleep, my daughter."

Cecily woke to a grove brimming with golden light, the sun low in the west. She stood and stretched, feeling restored. She couldn't see Aveta, but the altar held food again.

After Dane and Cecily had given thanks to the Goddess, and eaten and drunk their fill, Aveta spoke, though without appearing. "Go now, my children, and when you have done what must be done, return here to me that I may send you safely home."

"We will," Dane said. "Our thanks to you, Lady, for all your gifts." He and Cecily bowed their heads to Aveta's altar, and then turned away. They stood in the living archway for a moment, and then, without a backward glance, passed from peace into chaos.

THE DOOR IN THE TREE

Chapter Eight

Outside the grove, the forest lay in darkness. The Kerrighans' evil wind circled them, yowling like an angry cat thwarted of its prey. Its stench was so bad that Cecily took her jersey from around her waist and tied it over nose and mouth, but the wind seemed unable to harm her or Dane. The ruby, though now a part of her body, glowed with a steady crimson light.

"Where do we go now?" Cecily asked.

"Back to the road, and then we'll find the Queen—or she'll find us."

They entered the tunnel path that would take them downhill to the road again, and to Cecily's relief, the evil wind did not follow. It was chilly now, and she put on her jersey.

At first they walked in silence, the rosy beams of the ruby lighting their way. Cecily was very conscious of Dane beside her, warm and solid and *human*. She felt increasingly grateful for his companionship, his strength and kindness, in this journey through a strange world.

Maybe it was the rare experience of receiving compassion from Aveta, but for the first time she felt some concern for Dane. How had his years of imprisonment here affected him?

She could not have asked it to his face, but the darkness made it easy for her to speak. "Dane, how has it been for you, trapped here while a stranger lives your life in your place?"

"Lonely."

In that simple word, Cecily heard echoes of years of anguish and frustration, followed by hopeless acceptance. Like her, he'd suffered the soul-killing solitude of living among those who didn't love or understand him. She marveled at the lack of bitterness or self-pity in his voice. *"There are good men as well as evil men,"* Aveta's voice in her head reminded her.

"You must have missed your family and your friends."

"My mother is all my family now. My father died when I was eighteen, the year before I was taken."

"I'm sorry," said Cecily. "I understand. Mine died when I was sixteen, and I'm not sure I would have survived if I'd lost him much earlier."

"You're a survivor, Cecily. Don't underrate yourself."

"You keep saying that," she remarked.

"That's because I don't like to hear you put yourself down. I have a lot of respect for you, Cecily. You're gentle and soft-spoken, but you're very strong too—stronger than I think you realize. There is a special kind of strength in flexibility, that lets you bend but not break."

Cecily laughed and blushed a little in the dark. "Very well, I won't speak ill of myself in your presence. But I don't want to speak of myself at all right now; I want to hear about you. So, I am sure you missed your mother—she looks like a wonderful woman. And your friends?"

"I didn't have any close friends. When I finished work at the smithy, I tended to go off on my own, walking or fishing. I was always a dreamer—a daydreamer, my father used to say."

"How did they treat you when they brought you here? Were they unkind?" Cecily asked.

"No, not at all. They made me feel like an honored guest, and endowed me with some of the Folk's talents, like fire-bringing. And I was the Queen's pet at first. She kept me beside her at feasting, and gave me rich gifts, such as a fine white horse for riding with the Hunt. Of course I was flattered. I was only a boy, in my prime of lust, and eager to bed her."

"And did you?" Cecily tried to keep her voice level. However unreasonably, the idea of Dane making love to this Queen, of which she had heard nothing good, annoyed her very much.

"No, I did not—but only by my very good luck."

"How was that?" Cecily hoped her relief didn't show in her voice.

"First, the Folk like to spin out their pleasures instead of seizing them all at once. Time moves slowly here, and after thousands of years of indulging all their slightest whims, I think they are easily bored. So she kept me at a distance, savoring my eagerness and frustration. Then, before she chose to take me, she was distracted somehow. I didn't know much about this world then, but it seemed to have something to do with the rubies. Whatever it was, it angered her and roused her to action. She called all her ruby-holders together and they rode away to the Kerrighans' biggest grove to engage in some kind of battle. They must not have prevailed, for when they returned her attendants were all exhausted, and she was beside herself with rage."

"Maybe your mother and the Circle were raising trouble for her, trying to find you and get you back."

"You may be right. Anyway, she had no more desire for me after that. She took Arawn to her bed instead. At the time I was foolishly hurt, but I've learned to be grateful."

"I'm so glad." Cecily's tone was heartfelt. "I remember you talking about what happens to mortal men and women the Folk take for their lovers. Who is

Arawn? One of the Old Powers, you said, but I don't know anything more about him."

"His realm is in the Underworld, and he rules War and Revenge."

"So she went to bed with Revenge." Cecily shivered a little. Then the ruby brightened, and she said firmly the words that came into her mind. "Love is stronger than revenge."

"My mother's love, do you mean?" Dane asked doubtfully.

"That, and…" She hesitated. "Friendship is a kind of love, too and I believe you and I are friends now. Together I know we can stand against her."

Dane stopped and stood still, as if startled by her words. They'd surprised her too. Cecily could hardly hear his quickened breathing over the pounding of her own heart.

Why did I say that, that we are friends? she asked herself, and answered in the same breath, *Because it's true.*

"Cecily, I am honored by your friendship."

She thought he wanted to say more, but she wasn't sure she was ready to hear it. She realized he must have sensed that, and held back. "And I am honored by yours," she replied.

The road, when they reached it, lay broad and bone-white under the full moon. Cecily and Dane stood in the branch-roofed tunnel, in no hurry to leave its shelter. They watched an owl swoop low on silent powerful wings and rise again with a tiny limp creature in its talons..

Cecily moved, and Dane put a hand on her arm to stop her. "Wait! Do you hear it?"

Cecily made out a distant clamor up the road. Her ruby flared up bright, and as the noise got closer, she realized it was made up of several different sounds: shouts, and baying dogs, the clanging of metal objects—weapons?—and the unshod hooves of many horses.

A horn blared suddenly, and Cecily felt the high wild sound surging through her blood and bones, goading her to movement. Was she the huntress in pursuit of her prey? Or was *she* herself the prey, fleeing in terror? She knew only the mindless urge to run.

All around them in the forest, other creatures *were* running. The road before them filled with a thundering tide of deer and rabbits, foxes and wolves and badgers, fierce wild boars with their sharp tusks. Innumerable small animals, mice and voles and hedgehogs, ran underfoot, all of them heading away from the horn.

"It's the Wild Hunt," said Dane.

Blindly Cecily reached for Dane's hand and held it tight. She would not run.

THE DOOR IN THE TREE

Chapter Nine

The Hunt drew near, a dark roiling mass with scattered points of light, all in pairs: eyes.

"I rode with the Hunt three times," Dane said. "It's a nasty experience, though there's little actual killing done. It's all about feeding on terror."

"I believe it," Cecily replied. "That horn terrifies me, and yet another part of me, against my will, takes a sick pleasure in the animals' fear."

"That's exactly how I felt, though I could never explain it so well to myself," Dane said. "The Hunt spoiled the glamour of this place for me. It made me sick."

The Hunt drew near, slavering red-eyed hounds as big as ponies in the lead. Then came satyrs with their goats' legs and cloven hoofs, and goats' horns above human-seeming faces, and other nightmarish mixtures of man and beast. Tall grey-haired hags strode among them, their hands stained with something dark. Behind them, clad in silk and soft leather, mounted on horses of surpassing beauty, rode the Folk. Loveliest of them all was Maeve on her white stallion.

Clad in flowing green with flame-red hair rippling down her back, the Queen wore the face of a young girl. Her eyes widened in surprise as she saw Dane and Cecily, and she reined her horse to a stop, the rest of the Hunt halting behind her. She smiled down at them, and something ancient and cold and utterly inhuman looked out of her emerald eyes.

Cecily's ruby blazed. She thought that only its heat kept her blood from running cold. She clung to Dane's hand, and felt a reassuring pressure in return.

"So, my pet," Maeve addressed Dane, "how do you like being back in your own shape? Do you not miss the speed and strength of the pooka form?"

"Your Majesty, I am a man," Dane replied, "no more, no less. I aspire to no form but my own."

"I see you have found yourself a friend of your own kind."

The Queen's tone, both lewd and sarcastic, angered as well as embarrassed Cecily, more for Dane's sake than her own. *He is not your pet, Lady, whatever you think, and I* am *his friend.*

"As for you, woman—" Maeve turned to Cecily, looking her up and down with unveiled contempt, and making Cecily feel every day of her thirty-six years—*which is ridiculous,* Cecily thought. *She may look seventeen, but she must be thousands of years old.*

Only Cecily's own anger kept her from cringing away from the icy flame of rage in the Queen's eyes when they rested on the ruby. "As for you, mortal who dares to wear a piece of my ruby, you pretend to be much greater than you are."

There was no good answer to that, and Cecily didn't attempt to make one. She bowed her head and, feeling ridiculous in her jeans, sank into a deep curtsey.

"Another piece of Aveta's meddling, I suppose. Doesn't she know her day is past?"

Cecily remained silent. It wasn't a question she could answer.

Suddenly Maeve was all affability. "I won't harm you, mortal. I'm glad you show me proper respect, but you may rise."

No, you won't harm me, Cecily thought defiantly, *because Aveta and the ruby defend me.*

"You are, after all, a guest in my realm, however you came here," Maeve continued, with a slight emphasis on "my."

The man beside her frowned, and his tall black horse fidgeted, as if the hand on its reins had tightened. Like Aveta, the Queen's companion had black hair, dark eyes and olive skin. There the resemblance ended. His mouth, above a spade-shaped beard, looked arrogant and cruel, and his eyes had a red spark deep within them. *Arawn*, thought Cecily.

He was dressed for war rather than hunting, in a leather tunic reinforced with chainmail, a kilt of broad overlapping strips of thick hide, a bronze breastplate, gauntlets, bronze armbands and high boots. Though he wore no helmet, a sword swung from his belt and he carried a shield embossed with a fearsomely-tusked wild boar whose hot piggy eyes were tiny rubies. *Pieces of* the *ruby*, Cecily thought with a shiver, as her eyes returned to Maeve.

Oblivious to her companion's displeasure, the Queen trilled a musical little laugh. "How *did* you come into this land, woman?"

"By Aveta's grace, your Majesty."

"Aveta again." Maeve shrugged. "Well, since you are here, I bid you welcome. I trust you've enjoyed yourself so far. Tell me, do you mean to make a long stay?"

Cecily answered politely but without hesitation. "Thank you, your Majesty, but no. Lovely as this land is, I believe I must return home soon. My son has need of me."

"Oh, very well." Cecily thought Maeve sounded annoyed, though she continued to smile. "In the meantime, is there any boon you crave of me?" The smile had a sardonic twist, as if the Queen laughed at some unpleasant joke known only to herself.

To Maeve's obvious surprise, Cecily accepted the offer. "Most gracious Majesty," she began, "I do ask a boon of you. Dane, as you may see, is no longer young, and, I believe, no longer enjoys your favor. When I return to our homeland, will you permit him to come with me?"

"Oho!" cried the Queen. "That is no small thing you ask. Even though I no longer desire him myself, I do not readily yield up any man who has once been mine."

"Your Majesty, if there is anything I can offer you in return, please tell me."

Cecily felt Dane's sudden increase in tension, as his hand gripped hers.

"Fine talking. You cannot give me the stone you wear, I know that," Maeve said sourly. "Will you accept a challenge, a testing of your strength, and thus entertain me a little?"

Dale's grip on her hand tightened, and he whispered urgently into her ear, "Cecily, no!"

She ignored him and curtseyed again. "As you will, your Majesty."

The Queen called out, "Horses!" and immediately a lackey led forward two saddled steeds. "Come, ride with me to my court. There we shall make trial of your courage. No harm to you, I swear it, just a small test of your strength of character, for my amusement. Time moves slowly here," she said, echoing Dane's earlier words. "Our pleasures are rich and many, but our lives are long, and betimes we crave the spice of novelty."

Dane helped Cecily mount, then swung himself up into his saddle. The Queen wheeled her horse around to face the way she had come, with

Arawn, still frowning, at her left hand. Dane and Cecily followed, and the others fell in behind.

The road stretched out before them, pale as snow under the moon, rising to high forlorn hilltops, falling to dusky glens. From the forest on either side came mysterious rustlings, the death cries of small animals, the hoot of an owl. Tree limbs cast black shadows on the white road, shadows like strange misshapen beings that danced at another tempo than the wind-tossed branches. Far away over the hills, a pack of wolves sang allegiance to the full moon.

On and on the galloping steed carried Cecily. Wonder at the fantastical scene they traversed warred with her fear of falling off. Of past and future she did not think at all.

As the company rode on, the satyrs, hags, hellhounds, and other nightmare creatures left them, slinking away into the forest, until only Dane and Cecily, the Queen and Arawn and their attendant lords and ladies went forward.

The road crested one last hill and then dropped to a valley, where it ended at a wall of dense thorns and richly perfumed white roses, towering high above the Folk on their horses. Cecily wondered if they'd have to jump the hedge, but at their approach the brambles drew apart to form a wide arch. The Queen and her consort rode in side by side, Dane and Cecily behind them.

The flower-bejeweled meadow within was unmistakably the Queen's court. Under moonlight and torchlight it lay bright as midday. Silken tents lined one side, and across the meadow stood a long table, with a row of carved chairs behind it, the two at the center taller and more ornate than the rest. Graceful couples danced on the lawn to the melodious but somehow uncanny music of a harp, three pipers and a tambour drum.

Maeve and Arawn dismounted and strolled toward the table. Dane and Cecily and the rest slid off their horses, which were led away by invisible hands through a gap in the hedge.

As two men drew Dane aside, a bevy of ladies approached Cecily. "Come with us, Lady," said one, clad in rose and silver—a girl, Cecily would have said, but for her eyes, as cold and ancient as the Queen's. "Come, rest and refresh yourself before your contest."

Cecily followed them to one of the tents, where she was glad to find a toilet, a box with an open wooden seat on top. It seemed to appear, shimmering a little, just as she entered the curtained cubicle, as if called into being for her use alone. Idly she wondered whether the Folk even had digestive functions.

Next the ladies offered Cecily soap, towels, warm water in a silver basin, and when she'd washed, they guided her to the largest tent, where a banquet was set forth: haunches of roast boar, a peacock with its tail feathers in place, unidentifiable meats in rich sauces, grilled fish, baskets of bread, silver cups of delicate creams and jellies, fruits that looked too glossy and perfect to be real.

Remembering Dane's words about the Folk's food, Cecily refused everything, though with regret, for she was hungry. When at last convinced that she'd take nothing, the ladies led her toward the Queen's table, indicating that she should stand a little distance away.

Maeve and Arawn sat in their tall chairs, the Lord of the Underworld forking bloody meat into his mouth with grim single-mindedness, while the Queen toyed with the wing of some small roast bird. Maeve now wore a gown of green velvet richly embroidered with gold and pearls. The low neckline revealed three rubies, set like Cecily's in their wearer's flesh.

Embroidered on Arawn's tunic was the same snarling boar that decorated his shield, the beast's eyes again rubies. Cecily wondered if he had rubies for every outfit—horrid thought!—or if the rubies had somehow migrated from his shield. To either side sat splendidly clad lords and ladies, and Cecily saw with dismay that three more ladies wore single rubies at their throats.

Her own ruby glowed in response to the presence of the others. She expected the stones worn by the Folk to brighten also, but they did not. All of them, even the Queen's, looked dark and dull, and a burst of anger and grief emanated from her gem, such as she imagined a lioness might feel on seeing her sisters in vile captivity.

Dane came to stand by her side. He took her hand and leaned close as if to whisper in her ear, but the Queen's voice forestalled him.

"So, mortals." Maeve glanced at their interlaced hands with a sneer. "Very touching—but you undertake this trial alone, woman." Taking an ivory wand from her sleeve, she pointed it at the grass by Cecily's feet. A near-invisible shimmer of heat came from the tip and where that beam touched earth, the grass shriveled and burned. Maeve moved the wand until she'd drawn a blackened circle about two meters across.

"So, woman, these are my terms. In this circle you will face three of my champions in turn. If you defeat them and stay in the circle, you and your *friend*"—again she sneered—"may freely depart. But if you once step outside the circle, you have failed, and both of you will remain here as long as I choose to keep you. Agreed?"

Dane whispered, "Cecily, don't do it. Don't throw away your chance to return home, just for my sake."

"You keep telling me not to underestimate myself, but you don't seem to have much faith in me," she said plaintively.

"I do, I do have faith in you—but I don't trust Maeve to honor her word if things don't go as she likes. If you just refuse to play, I don't think she can keep you here."

"Dane, listen. For the first time in my life, I have faith in myself. I believe I can stand up to anything she throws at me. Besides, I'm not sure Maeve would let me go even if I did leave you behind." Half to herself, she added, "And I don't want to leave you behind."

Dane's hand tightened on hers. "Cecily, what can I do?"

"Watch me, and wish me well. That will help." She pulled her hand gently away, kissed his cheek, and stepped into the circle Maeve had drawn. "Agreed" she said.

Chapter Ten

As Cecily waited to see what Maeve would throw at her, a tidings of magpies flew over the hedge and fanned out to settle just outside the ring of charred grass. Cecily's heart lifted at the sight of them, hoping they meant that Dane's mother and her Circle were somehow working to aid her.

Maeve looked at them with disfavor. "What do you here, vermin fowl? Why do you intrude in my court?"

The magpies gave her beady-eyed stares, and the largest spoke, hoarsely but distinctly. "We are here to see fair play."

Maeve still held the wand, and she raised it a little, as though to blast them, but the birds stared at her, unblinking, until she lowered her hand and tucked the wand away in her sleeve.

Arawn looked at Maeve without expression, and for the first time in Cecily's hearing he spoke, his voice harsher and less human-sounding than the magpie's. "Magic has rules," he said, and when Maeve turned to glare at him, he added with a faint, malicious smile, "Even yours."

Maeve, as if she hadn't heard, glanced around at her assembled lords and ladies and smiled sweetly. Besides those seated at her table, all the others who'd been dancing on the lawn or reclining in tents with plates of food now gathered in a loose circle around

Cecily's tiny arena. Even the musicians stopped playing and came to watch.

"Are you ready?" she asked Cecily.

"I am."

As the words left her lips, she was no longer alone in the circle. Her mother stood facing her, much younger and more vigorous than Cecily had seen her last. The ruby's glow and heat told her that what she saw was produced by magic, but the face before her didn't change. Before she could try to puzzle out what this meant, her mother burst into speech.

"What the hell do you think you're doing here, you stupid little bitch? Look at you, like a teenager in your completely unsuitable blue jeans, pretending you're good enough to face the Queen. Ridiculous.

You've always been feeble and useless, daydreaming your life away."

Cecily wilted under the lash of her mother's words, as though she was fifteen years old, or five, a timid despairing child again. She felt the scornful eyes of Maeve's court upon her, endorsing her mother's judgment, and confidence seeped away, replaced by misery.

"You can't do anything right, can you?" the scathing voice went on, as the face—so classically lovely of feature, so marred and twisted with ugly emotion—came closer and closer to Cecily's. "You were mediocre at best in school, and brought discredit to our name with your unfortunate tendency to socialize with the lower orders."

Rather than stinging as it was meant to, this remark heartened Cecily a little by reminding her of Dane. She thought she could sense a small but helpful inflow of strength from where he stood behind her, opposing the negative energy of the other onlookers. Her mother's next remarks, however, struck hard.

"You couldn't make a success of marriage, either, could you? What good did your fine American husband do you? You came trotting home with your tail between your legs like the worthless little bitch you are, and here you are, still dependent on me."

Her face was only inches away now, and Cecily found herself stepping backward to avoid the spittle flying from the angry mouth. As always, she had no response to her mother's contempt but silent endurance.

"And wearing *my* ruby too," Laetitia Moreton's voice continued. "Don't imagine it will do you any good, you useless good-for-nothing slut."

But the magpies' loud voices drowned out the last words. Seven of them rose and flew around Cecily's head—and she remembered the vision in Aveta's chalice.

"The ruby was never yours," she said. "The Circle took it away before it could pass into your hands, because you were too arrogant to hold it. It was my grandmother's, and now it is mine. As for you, you have no superior wisdom, and I grant you no more authority over me. I ignore you." With these words she turned her back on her mother.

Behind her she heard an angry squawk ring out, and then nothing. Dane caught her eye and raised a fist with his thumb held upright. She grinned and turned to face the Queen again—and saw that she now stood alone in the circle.

The sour look on Maeve's otherwise lovely face reminded Cecily of her mother as a young woman. "So," the Queen said coldly. "Are you ready for my next champion?"

The next challenger wore Drew's face—again, as with her mother, much younger than his present age.

"Mom, you're ruined my whole life." The childish treble voice quavered with misery. The last time Drew said those words, he'd spoken so insolently that he'd roused her anger, and made it easy for her to dismiss the accusation. But instead of a sulky, defiant teenager, this Drew looked no more than nine years old. At that age he'd still let her cuddle him sometimes, and he looked so sad and vulnerable that she longed to take him in her arms.

"I had no choice, sweetie," she said, aching to comfort him, but despising the weakness in her voice. "There were reasons why we couldn't stay in Seattle." *But maybe it's true,* she thought, as she watched tears gather in his eyes. Maybe she *had* ruined his life—not by leaving his father and bringing him to England, but by staying with his father as long as she had, letting an abuser be his role model, raising her son in a climate of lies and fear.

She'd always felt this underlying guilt about Drew's upbringing, she realized, and she could feel it sapping her strength now. "I know England is still strange to you, but you'll soon make new friends here," she said in a soothing tone. " You are half-English, after all."

"Yeah, the shitty half!" His lip curled with scorn, reminding her unbearably of her mother. "I don't *want* to be English—like *you*." He almost spit. "I want to go back to my father. I hate you! You're ugly and mean and stupid, and pathetic, and I hate you."

Cecily's eyes filled with tears. Hearing those words, from the only person in the whole world she loved, made her want to howl with grief. She turned her back and took one stumbling tear-blinded step away from him.

Suddenly the magpies arose and flew around the meadow, making the spectators duck their heads in alarm. Four of the birds swooped back down to stand in a little row at the edge of circle facing Cecily. *Four for a boy*, she thought automatically, and at the same time she heard Dane's voice in her head saying, "Kids that age hate everybody, especially their mothers."

It's not just memory bringing those words to my head, she thought. *It's Dane, sending me courage and common sense with all the strength of his will.* She raised her head to meet his eyes, and mouthed a silent "Thank you" before she turned back to Drew.

"That's enough," she said, firmly but without heat. "Yes, you've seen me treated without respect by others, but that gives you no right to be disrespectful to me yourself."

"My father— " he began.

"Your father never cared if you lived or died. Why do you think he let you go with me?"

In spite of the boy's stricken look, she knew she'd been right. Those words had to be said. "Your father provided you with material comforts, and nothing else," she said. "I, not he, loved you, cared for you, comforted you, encouraged you, fostered your talents and intelligence. Maybe you don't love me. I accept that. No one can love on command. But you do owe me respect and gratitude."

The ruby pulsed with crimson light at her throat. Whether it reflected that light, or whether from embarrassment, the accusing face of the boy facing her grew red as well.

"Furthermore, I have not ruined your life. Many children have experienced far worse than anything you've ever suffered, and gone on to make good lives for themselves. If you choose to sulk and whine about your changed circumstances instead of living your life where you are, the blame is yours." To her own ears the words sounded harsh, but the sting was medicinal, she knew. She spoke them in love, for her son's good and her own, and she felt Dane's approval at her back.

The vivid red faded slowly from the boy's face. Then before her eyes the boy grew transparent—and vanished. Once more Cecily stood alone in the ring, victorious but bewildered.

That apparition could not have truly been her son, any more than the previous image had truly been her mother—especially since both appeared several years younger than their real age—and yet her ruby hadn't dispelled those visions, nor shown her anything else in their place.

By Cecily's reckoning, that made each of her challengers both truth and illusion. How could that be? But she was given no more time to ponder the question.

"Are you ready for the next challenge?" asked the Queen, with a look of anticipation, almost gloating.

"I am," Cecily said—and stood face to face with her ex-husband.

Philip was an attractive man of thirty-five—again, years younger than when Cecily had last seen him—with handsome features, dark eyes, smooth dark hair, and a carefully tended, athletic body. At first glance his smile looked genuine.

"Little Cecily," he greeted her in a caressing tone. "I've missed you. Now, why, why did I ever let you leave me?"

"Because if you'd refused to let me go, I would have taken you to court, and had subpoenas sent to every doctor who treated me during our marriage. I understood why you'd rarely let me see the same doctor twice, but you couldn't stop me from remembering their names. The cumulative effect of their testimony would have destroyed your good name, even if I'd lost my case. My body bears too many scars, too many of them in intimate places. Your only alternative would have been to kill me, and that too would have ruined your standing in the community. Even if you went free in the end, you couldn't have escaped standing your trial. But I said I wouldn't accuse you if you'd just let me leave with Drew, and you consented."

"Such a literal-minded little thing." The smile still clung to his lips, but his eyes narrowed in anger. "So you see me as the cruel abuser, and yourself as the innocent victim?"

"Yes, of course I do."

"Oh, no, no, no, my little Cecily, it's not that simple. It was never that simple. You put yourself in my power voluntarily, remember?"

"Before I knew you. That was stupid, I know, but I trusted you once."

"And then you stayed. I beat you and raped you and tortured you and degraded you, over and over again—and you stayed."

"Because I was afraid to leave—and then Drew was born, and I was even more afraid to risk his life by trying to escape you."

An airy wave of Philip's hand dismissed Drew as irrelevant. "Nonsense. You stayed because you liked what I did to you."

Cecily wasn't sure if the gasp of outrage was her own—or Dane's. Maybe it was both. "That's bullshit, and you know it."

"Oh, such nasty language from the demure little Englishwoman." Philip laughed. "No, my dear, it's not, and *you* know it. You'd never known anything in your genteel, dreary little life as thrilling as the sex games I thought up for us. God, how I loved the way you screamed."

"I screamed in pain and terror, not in orgasm." Cecily had passed beyond any shame at what Philip revealed of their life together. "You know that. Anyway, you wouldn't recognize a woman's orgasm if it bit you. Neither would I, for that matter."

"Dear little Cecily, you're being rather disingenuous here, aren't you? Yes, I know I inflicted pain on you—but you *wanted* all that pain and degradation. You asked for it."

"That's not true! No one asks to be treated the way you treated me."

"Oh my dear, you're such a limp, useless, naïve little thing. A girl like you is a walking invitation to abuse. All I did was accept the invitation."

"Yes, I was naïve. I didn't know what you were when I married you. But that doesn't mean I wanted any of the things you did to me."

"Look inside yourself, my dear," Philip said, with a smug, knowing half-smile. "You consented to it, all of it. You crave punishment because you know you deserve it."

Cecily stared into his eyes. They were smiling, as she had so often seen them, savoring her humiliation. She felt ashamed, not because of how he'd used her, but because she felt the truth of what he'd just said. She'd never desired any of the things he did to her, but believing that she deserved no better, she had, for fourteen long years, tacitly consented to his abuse.

She looked away from the triumph in his eyes as he watched her, and saw Maeve staring at her with salacious enjoyment, licking her lips as if she tasted something delicious. Heart sinking under the weight of shame, she dropped her eyes to the grass at her feet.

"Yes, little Cecily," Philip crooned. "You are still mine, still my pretty little slave girl." He took two steps forward to where Cecily stood mesmerized by fear, and reached out to touch her breast. "Such delicious memories I have of your submission." He pinched her nipple sharply.

She wrenched out of his grasp, and turned and stumbled away from him. The ruby flared at her throat, and the magpies rose and circled her with hoarse cries before they settled right at the edge of the circle. Cecily halted, looking down at the charred grass so close to her feet, and took a deep breath. She would not yield, she would never yield to him again.

Her back was to Philip still, but in her mind she confronted him—and confronted the problem of how he could be here and not here, truth and illusion at the same time, just as her mother and her son had been both truth and illusion.

There was no time limit in her bargain with the Queen, so she would stand here with her back to the problem for as long as she needed to, and she would *think*. She could sense Dane's support blending with the warmth of the ruby, and the largest of the magpies plucked a feather from its own tail and pushed it across the burnt grass toward Cecily.

She picked it up, heartened. *Courage*, she remembered, and she went on thinking.

"You consented." That was the key.

It was true, and not true—just as Philip behind her was both here and not here.

Maeve hadn't brought those three here in truth from their own time, taken years off their ages. Yet the ruby showed her nothing in their place, so Maeve had not disguised any minions of hers as Cecily's mother and son and ex-husband. Real and not real, truth and illusion...

"You consented." She *had* consented to her mother's emotional abuse, to Drew's guilt trips, to Philip's perverse cruelties—not openly, not verbally, but inside herself. Why?

Because, as Philip said, she hadn't believed she deserved any better. But how could she possibly have thought that she deserved guilt and pain and humiliation?

Because they had told her so. All her life there had been someone to tell her she was worthless, and not knowing any better, she'd believed them. Her father had done what he could for her, but they'd spent too little time together, and Cecily doubted that he'd seen the full extent of her mother's willful destruction of their child's spirit.

No more. Maybe it was because somehow, on her own, she *had* found the courage to leave both abusers, and the courage to confront Drew's disrespect. Maybe it was Aveta's compassion, and especially Dane's friendship—proof that some people didn't despise her. Maybe it was the ruby: not just having it, but having been given it, having been chosen to possess it. Probably it was all these things. But she knew now that she was far from worthless, and she would no longer permit anyone to tell her so, or treat her so.

Her challengers were real and not real, truth and illusion, she understood now, because they wore the faces of the people who lived inside her, poisoning her confidence. For too long she'd internalized her abusers' messages. But she would give them a place in her soul no longer. Knowing them for phantoms, she could refuse them her consent. Their power wouldn't vanish overnight, she knew, but as she continued to resist, in time they'd lose their hold on her.

Cecily turned to face the wraith that wore Philip's face. "You are not true. You are only an illusion, a lie I refuse to accept. I no longer give you belief or consent. I will not give you the satisfaction of my fear. The time will come when I won't even remember you, for months and then for years on end. You are nothing." She pointed a finger at him, confident as if she held Maeve's wand of power. "Begone," she said, and he vanished.

Her ruby blazed up bright as a bonfire, and the magpies rose in a cloud to wheel around her head, uttering hoarse cries of triumph. She thought she heard Dane shouting too.

Cecily raised her eyes to Maeve's cold stare. "I have won," she said.

Maeve shook off Arawn's hand, which rested on her arm as if to restrain her. "You have won," she said acidly. She pointed her wand at the charred ring of grass and it grew fresh and green again. "Now, go,

both of you, before I change my mind."

Chapter Eleven

The magpies led the way to the gate, Cecily and Dane stumbling hand in hand after them. Her victory acknowledged, Cecily's energy had drained away entirely, and Dane was in little better condition—because, Cecily realized, he'd given so much of his strength to her.

Once outside, the birds veered away from the road into a narrow woodland track, pausing to look back at the humans and utter encouraging caws.

"I think they know a shortcut," Cecily guessed—and in a very few minutes they arrived at Aveta's grove, entering not by the green tunnel they'd used before, but slipping between two great spreading oaks into an opening near the altar.

Again the altar was laden with simple but plentiful food. Cecily and Dane drank their fill of pure water, and then collected fruit, bread, and cheese, and sat down on the moss to eat in silent comradeship, too exhausted for speech.

The magpies left their perches around the edge of the grove to hop across the moss and peck at crumbs. In silent agreement, Cecily and Dane tossed bits of cheese in the birds' direction.

Cecily spoke at last. "I feel like I've known you all my life, Dane."

Dane answered, "Well, you have, pretty much. What were we, five years old when we first met?" He yawned suddenly and hugely.

"Don't do that!" Cecily cried. "I'm sleepy too, but we have to go back as soon as we possibly can. I have no idea how long I've been away. Drew must be frantic."

"And your mother?"

"Probably having kittens by now, but I don't care anymore."

Aveta's voice spoke nearby, though she did not appear. "Sleep without fear, my daughter. When I send you back to your time, you will arrive only a few hours after you left home."

"And Dane?"

"Dane will be with you."

"After all we've been through together, Dane, I don't want to lose track of you."

"You won't," he said. "I promise."

Cecily slept without dreams on the soft moss that carpeted Aveta's grove, and woke to see Dane sitting up and rubbing his eyes a little distance away.

They looked at each other for a long moment without speaking. Cecily thought, *I want to spend the rest of my life with you, Dane.*

He smiled as tenderly as though he'd heard her, and felt the same.

Cecily didn't think she'd said it out loud. She wasn't quite ready to do that yet, but she would be soon. Aloud she said, "Thank you for your support, Dane, when I was facing— them. I could feel you sending me strength. You must have been as exhausted as I was afterwards."

"I was glad to be able to help," he said. Then he burst out, "My God, you're strong, Cecily! How you survived such a mother, and then such a husband, I can't begin to imagine."

"My father loved me. He was a quiet man, but I knew he valued me, and so I must have known somewhere inside me I was not quite as worthless as the others said. He taught me to think logically, too, and that helped me win in the end. Once I got past the shame of realizing I *had* consented to my own abuse, I understood that my ghosts had only whatever power I gave them by believing in them—and so I stopped believing. With your help."

"Getting past the shame of consent—that's a hard thing to do. I have some of that to deal with myself. Not that I ever suffered such horrendous abuse as you did, but every time I remember how I let Maeve seduce me in taking part in the Hunt and some of the other perverse pleasures of her court, I feel dirty all over." His lip curled in self-disgust.

"Don't be too hard on yourself," Cecily said. "You were very young, and alone in a strange land. It must have been hard to believe you'd ever escape."

"As hard as it must have been for you, when you were married to that— *thing*."

Cecily shuddered, and then said firmly, "It's all behind us now."

"Yes," Dane said. "Here we are, together, and soon we will be back home in Stow."

Suddenly one of the magpies rose up and flew away. It was Elinor's magpie, Cecily thought—the largest, the one that spoke sometimes, the one that had given her the ruby.

"Maybe he's gone to tell your mother we're coming home," Cecily said.

"Maybe so. I can believe anything now." He smiled, a joyous smile that made her heart turn over.

She said softly, "I wish…".

"What do you wish, dear heart?"

"When we get back, I want us to stay together."

"So do I." Dane stood and crossed the brief distance separating them to kneel beside her. "Cecily, I love you. Will you marry me?"

"I will."

They kissed like loving children, in innocence and tenderness.

Aveta spoke in the air nearby. "I bless your union, my children. Come, it is time for you to bathe in my pool and be cleansed of all your sins and sorrows."

The rest of the magpies flew away, and Cecily and Dane undressed.

Now he will see all my scars, Cecily thought, and then, *So what? He has seen the scars on my soul already. He knows me and loves me for who I am.*

When both stood naked, they looked at each other, a long steady look of peaceful acceptance, and then hand in hand, they stepped into Aveta's healing waters.

Time stopped. As the cool sweet water poured into the pool from the sacred spring, and drained away into the moss, Cecily felt every ill she'd ever suffered, of body or spirit, floating away from her. Every despairing thought vanished, every evil memory grew dim and distant.

When she emerged, she was surprised that her body still wore its scars. *But they're like the bad memories—they'll never vanish entirely, but they'll never hurt me or shame me again.*

Cecily stood dripping on the moss, seeing Dane in a new way. She eyed his nakedness with pleasure and curiosity, and a set of physical responses she'd never imagined flooded her body. Dane's own physical response to the sight of her was plain to see.

He took her in his arms, and they kissed again, not as children kiss...

When they had made love, and rested, and reluctantly gotten dressed again, Aveta appeared behind her altar.

"Now you are one flesh," she said. "When you are home again, you may be wed by the rites of your time and place, but here you have sealed your true marriage."

Cecily and Dane bowed to the Goddess in silent thanksgiving.

"Now go to your tree, my daughter, and the door will open for you."

Chapter Twelve

Cecily and Dane emerged into the soft glow of Stow's old-fashioned streetlights. Night had fallen, but Cecily trusted Aveta's word that it was the same evening she'd left home.

Dane stood looking around him in some bewilderment, and Cecily understood. She felt bewildered herself, and she'd only been in Fairyland, or whatever it was, for a day or two. Dane had been there nearly half his life, and now here he stood on an ordinary Twenty-First Century city street. At least it was a quiet street, she thought gratefully.

She looked down the neck of her jersey at the ruby imbedded in her flesh. To her relief it lay dim and quiescent. Beams of red light from her body would be hard to explain here.

A uniformed policeman rounded the corner and stopped at the sight of them. "Miss Moreton, isn't it?"

"Yes, sir."

"I'm glad to see you, miss. Your mother is… a trifle concerned about your absence."

"Oh, indeed?" Dane asked politely. He winked at Cecily.

"Yes, sir, Mr. Blacksmith. It seems she called the station about an hour ago to say that her daughter had 'flung out of the house in some kind of fit.' So I went along to the residence, and Mrs. Moreton tried to tell me that Miss here was mentally ill."

Cecily saw Dane's mouth open in protest and silenced him with a gesture. "Really?" she asked politely. "I can assure you I am not."

"I believe you, miss. As far as I could see, Mrs. Moreton was the one who'd thrown a fit. There was a mess of food and broken dishes on the floor, and when I asked her who had done it, well, she opened her mouth to tell me a lie, I believe, and she saw the boy—your son, miss?"

Cecily nodded.

"Anyway, she saw the boy looking at her, and she shut her mouth like a steel trap."

"Did she, now?" asked Dane in a satisfied tone.

"She did, and I never had another word out of her. So I told her I'd go out and take a look around for you, and she was not to worry, I was sure you'd turn up safe and sound. Then I told the boy he'd best clean up the floor before you got home, and when he protested that he didn't make the mess, I said, 'I know that, your granny did it, but *she* won't clean it up, and if you don't, it'll be left for your poor mum, and she's had enough to bear.' Such a startled look as he gave me, you'd think it had never occurred to him to do anything to spare his mother trouble!"

"I don't think it *has* ever occurred to him," Cecily said ruefully. "That's as much my fault as anyone's, but change is in the air."

"Very good, miss. I'll be saying goodnight now, wishing you both a pleasant evening."

Dane laughed as he and Cecily watched the officer's uniformed back recede up the street. "I wish

I'd seen your son's face when our friend told *him* to clean up the mess."

"So do I," she said. "Oh, so do I. Well, let's go." She paused. "That is, do you want to come with me now, or would you rather go home?"

"Oh, I'm coming with you. I wouldn't miss it for anything. Besides, I'm not sure what happens next for me. Has the changeling already vanished in a puff of smoke, or will I have to confront him? One thing at a time, that's my thinking. Let's go."

Chapter Thirteen

Cecily turned her key in the front door's lock, and apart from the polished grandfather clock in the hall striking the half-hour, heard only silence. The clock, astonishingly, showed only 8:30.

In the parlor there was no sign of Drew. Cecily's mother sat rigid and stone-faced in her wheelchair. She looked up at Cecily's entrance, frowned at the sight of Dane, and said, "So you're back."

"Yes, for now."

"And what do you mean by that, may I ask?"

Cecily kept her voice matter-of-fact. Her intent was not to accuse, but to state her limits. "I mean that I won't put up with you cursing me and throwing things any longer. If you wish me to remain here, you will speak to me with simple courtesy. If you feel you can't manage that, then hire someone else or go into a nursing home. It's up to you. In any case, I'll be leaving soon to get married, so you may as well start thinking about what you want to do next."

"Married? You?"

"Yes, me. I'll give you three weeks' notice— if you want me to stay that long." She stood looking at her mother, seeing in her withered face the ghost of the young woman she'd once been, and wondering what had gone wrong with her.

"I'm curious, Mother. You've despised me all my life, hated me really, from before I was old enough for you to have any idea what my talents or my personality might be. Why?"

The old woman's mouth worked as though she was chewing on something bitter, and her eyes filled with angry tears. "I never wanted a girl," she burst out. "Girls are useless. I wanted a son who'd take his place in the great world, who'd develop all his talents and powers as I was never permitted to do."

"Mother, what century are you living in?" cried Cecily, astonished. "Women can do anything they want to do now. We've had a woman Prime Minister."

"A woman, yes," her mother said scathingly. "Not a *lady*."

"Thank God I'm not a lady, then."

Her mother looked her up and down with distaste. "No, you certainly are not."

"And you are? Is it ladylike to throw your supper on the floor like a toddler in a tantrum? Or to abuse your daughter from her infancy in language that would make a sailor blush?"

"You've driven me to it."

"No."

"No, what?" Her mother stared, whether more angered or amazed by the bald defiance of that syllable, Cecily could not tell.

"No, it's not about me. It's never been about me. I'm sorry you felt you couldn't achieve anything because you were a girl, but that is not my fault. You've been stewing in your bitterness since before I was born. It's long past time to stop blaming me for everything you don't like about your life, and take responsibility for your own ugly emotions."

Mrs. Moreton began to make the gobbling noise that usually preceded one of her tirades.

Cecily looked at her dispassionately. "Before you throw another tantrum, Mother, let's get one thing clear. I will take no further abuse from you. I refer to verbal abuse, since no matter how hard you try, you no longer have the power to inflict emotional abuse on me. If you begin to curse at me again, I will leave. Drew and I will go to a hotel, tonight."

No one spoke for some minutes. Only the clock striking the quarter hour broke the silence.

The old woman spoke first. "I suppose you plan to marry this... this *peasant* you've brought in with you." She seemed to have accepted defeat, for she sounded merely querulous instead of violently angry.

"That's right." Cecily grinned. "I told you, I'm not a lady."

"I don't want him in my house."

"Very well then. I'll need to insist on my formal times off, which I haven't bothered to do before. I'll say goodnight to Dane now, and then I'll help you get ready for bed. Tomorrow we can discuss the timing of my breaks."

Outside the front door under the portico, Cecily and Dane embraced. She said wistfully, "I'll see you tomorrow, love."

"Yes, you will," Dane said into her ear. "Tomorrow we'll go ask the vicar of St Edwards to start calling the banns for our wedding."

Cecily felt a warmth below her throat, and a rosy glow seeped through her jersey, as a tall blonde woman approached the garden gate. It was Dane's mother, she saw, and felt suddenly shy.

"Oh my dears, I am so glad to see you both at last." Elinor hugged her son, then turned to embrace Cecily with equal fervor. "Dane, I knew you were safe back when the thing that wore your shape turned into a wren and flew away. Wrens are the Druids' birds, you know, so the Kerrighans use them as messengers."

She turned to Cecily again, with a beaming smile. "And you, Cecily—oh my dear, we've waited so long to welcome you, we of the Circle. We would have given you the ruby years ago, if you'd been within our reach. Please come to LunaGold tomorrow afternoon. Several of us will be there, and we're so looking forward to getting to know you. You did so well against Maeve! We're all longing to hear how you did it."

Cecily glowed with more than the ruby's warmth, with more even than her love for Dane. At last she was valued and welcomed and praised. At last she had a community. With a light heart she hugged Elinor again, kissed Dane, and went inside to deal with her mother.

In the downstairs room that had been Cecily's father's study and now contained a hospital bed, her mother was cold but polite, and to Cecily's surprise, quite capable of getting herself ready for bed. Previously she'd been too feeble—or so it had seemed—to lift her arms and legs, and Cecily had been forced to dress her like a doll.

Tonight, though she sometimes paused to sit on the edge of the bed for a moment, Cecily's mother undressed and put on her nightgown without assistance.

"Since you no longer need help dressing," Cecily said calmly, "I suggest you consider a man for your next caregiver. He might irritate you less than a woman."

Her mother grunted.

Cecily said goodnight and went upstairs in search of Drew. As she'd expected, she found him lying on his bed with earbuds in place, reading *anime* comics. He looked up, and she saw with compunction that his eyes were red. *He must have been crying.*

"So you're back," he said gruffly.

"Of course I'm back. Did you think I'd leave you?"

He lowered his eyes, and she realized he hadn't been sure.

"I would never leave you, Drew. I love you."

"You left my father, for no good reason."

"I had a good reason. Do you want to know why I left him?"

Until now Cecily had met his questions with vague nothings about incompatibility. She thought now that it might have been a mistake to shield Drew from the truth.

Drew looked startled "Yeah, I guess."

"I left because I couldn't let him beat me anymore."

He looked her in the eye with a challenging stare that said, "Yeah, right."

"When I was pregnant with what would have been your sister, he kicked me in the belly until I miscarried. In the last three years alone of our marriage he broke my nose, my collarbone, both arms and my jaw—and the abuse was escalating. When he almost ruptured my kidneys, I knew I had to get out."

"I don't believe you!" His look of naked shock said, "I don't *want* to believe you."

"You must have noticed how often I was injured."

Drew lowered his eyes.

He's ashamed, thought Cecily. *Good.* Of course he'd noticed. He just hadn't wanted to think about it. He'd accepted without question all her lame explanations for bruises and broken bones, and shrugged when she'd muttered that she must be accident prone. He'd only noticed her condition when it affected his own needs—as when she was too badly injured to chauffeur him.

She watched memories and emotions chase each other across his face, truth and illusion struggling for supremacy. For all his thirteen years, he was still transparent as a child.

"I know it's hard to accept, Drew. It wasn't easy for me to accept that I'd married an abuser. At first I told myself he really did love me; he was under a lot of stress; it was my fault for not handling him right—all the things battered women do tell themselves. But I finally saw that he'd chosen me, a naïve girl with no family, and brought me to America where no one knew me, because there'd be no one to ask questions about how he treated me."

"Why didn't you leave earlier?" The note of challenge left his voice, replaced by appalled curiosity.

"I was afraid he'd kill me if I tried to leave, and when you were little, I was afraid for your sake too."

"So how come you did finally leave?"

"Partly because the abuse was getting worse— and partly because I finally understood that hurting me was a calculated pleasure for him, not truly a compulsion. Killing me would have meant the end of his reputation and his social standing, and they mattered more to him than I did. When I said he'd have to choose, he chose to keep his lifestyle, and let you and me go."

"Why didn't you fight him in court?" It was a child's cry of outrage, of "it's not fair!"

"If I'd done that, he *would* have killed me. He'd have had nothing left to lose."

Drew burst into tears. "Mommy, Mommy, I'm sorry. I didn't know. I've been so awful to you. Tonight I was afraid you'd left me—and I wouldn't have blamed you."

Cecily sat on the bed and put her arms around him. "I'd never leave you, Drew. Some of this is my fault; I should've told you earlier instead of letting you think I was just being selfish when I left him. I was ashamed—but I'm not ashamed any more. We'll have a better life soon, I promise. Your grandmother has been a poisonous influence on our lives, and we'll be moving out in a few weeks."

"But, but, how— ?"

"That's for tomorrow, sweetie. I need my sleep, and so do you. Go wash your face and brush your teeth, and then I'll tuck you up in bed."

A watery but impish smile dawned on the boy's tear-stained face. "And will you read to me too? Please, Mommy! Read *Where the Wild Things Are*?"

"I'll give you Wild Things, kiddo. You tossed that book out when you were ten." She laughed and ruffled his hair. "I'm not going to sing *Rock-a-bye Baby* either—but I *will* tuck you up and kiss you goodnight. Go on now. Scoot. I'll wait for you here."

Cecily lay in her bed at last, in the lovely pale green paneled bedchamber that had been hers in childhood. She'd always been grateful her mother hadn't realized that being confined to her room was no punishment. Alone with her books and her dolls, and the graceful willow tree outside the window, she'd felt safe and happy. Not quite alone, either, for there had always been magpies outside the window, chattering to her, making her laugh with their antics. *Keeping an eye on me for the Circle*, she guessed, *until I was old enough to wear the ruby.*

Her thoughts drifted across her childhood, remembering the good...

Walks in the woods with her father... sitting by the fire with him when her mother was out... quaint old books in the library... the fascination of history... her schooldays...

I dreamed about Dane in this bed, when I was sixteen. Recalling the dream, she blushed, for it had been most erotic, and then she laughed to herself. *I'll dream of him again tonight.*

And tomorrow.

ABOUT THE AUTHOR

Alison Jean Ash has loved bookstores and libraries all her nomadic life. Her many jobs, besides writing and parenthood, included seven years working in shelters for homeless women and men. Happily settled in the Pacific Northwest with her sexy book-loving husband, Alison enjoys reading, swimming, camping in a yurt at the coast, spoiling her grandchildren, and being a soccer hooligan.

Please visit http://arachnealison.blogspot.com/ and https://www.facebook.com/authorAlisonAsh for more about Alison. And if you enjoyed this story, please consider reviewing it on amazon.com.

Made in the USA
San Bernardino, CA
25 November 2015